CW01003846

'The Polestars'
by
David Giblin

Carl Ross Publishing

Published by Carl Ross Publishing
P.O. Box 268, Sproatley, HU11 4WJ
crp@gibwinn.karoo.co.uk

First printed November 2008

ISBN Number 978-0-9559208-0-6

For my sister Pat, a true star in the night sky and to my wife Janet and sons Ross and Carl who make everything worthwhile.

With thanks to Brian Gosling for his work on Illustration and Neil Mace for Graphics/Page Design.

Introduction

High above the surface of the Earth, but closer to the North Pole than any other star, lies the beautiful Polaris. Due to its present geographical location, Polaris is known as a Pole Star and is one of several stars to have held this title along with others such as Thurban, Alrai, Aldermin, Vega and Kochab.

Unbeknown to mankind, Pole Stars are inhabited by billions of tiny life forms called............Polestars, with similar but exaggerated characteristics to humans. However, one quite unique characteristic to Polestars is that they glow in the dark. This is the reason why their stars shine so brightly at night when viewed from Earth. What you are actually seeing are billions of Polestars 'glowing about their business.'

Not only do Polestars glow in the dark, they glow different colours depending upon which star they come from. Polestars from Polaris for example, glow yellow, whilst those from Aldermin and Kochab glow white and orange respectively.

The personalities and behaviours of Polestars also differ depending upon their star of origin. Those from Thurban are pure diplomats with a firm belief that the word is more powerful than the sword. Polestars from Alrai and Kochab however, are more likely to take up arms to defend a cause, with Kochab in particular seeing much internal disruption in the past. Today it has become the much respected guardian of Polaris.

As with all forms of life, survival is dependent upon securing resources that sustain and help us to grow and develop. The existence of Polestars is totally attributed to the acquisition and ingestion of 'Istella', which is now only found in a village in the East of England known as Sproatsville.

Thousands of years ago, deep in space, the large star Stella G exploded, sending asteroids and comet particles into the far corners of the universe. A very large asteroid penetrated the Earth's natural solar defences, massively impacting upon Holderness and in particular Sproatsville. This rendered the area rich in comet debris, which, when crushed, releases the ancient glowing space dust Istella.

Every lunar month, Polestars visit Sproatsville on assignment to harvest Istella as they have done for thousands of years. A community and social structure now exists alongside humans, who, all but for one, don't know they exist.

This book captures the adventures and challenges of some of the Polestars who make the journey to Earth through the gravity corridor, facing the perils of Red Snapper, a mutant Polestar exiled in Sproatsville, and their arch intergalactic enemies the Frombrasent Welps.

Their journeys are crammed with excitement, trauma, humour and grief in their search for Istella and the ultimate prize, the 'magical and mystical Auwnwanx.'

Chapter One

Never ending, black and speckled with space dust, was the only description Ripbag could provide when surveying the awesome space between Polaris and the millions of other twinkling stars the night had exposed. Oh, and freezing cold too he thought, as he brought his head back into position. He was certainly right about that. It was the sort of evening where one's breath resembles that of a dragon puffing out plumes of smoke from each nostril.

Standing at the highest point on Polaris, Ripbag was able to look down on the land before him and see its radiance light up the universe. One couldn't fail to be impressed by the glow generated by Polestars going about their daily business. Not that Ripbag was impressed, he was actually bored, and as a result was sucking on his finger taking in a deep breath and then exhaling. He had seen this odd behaviour during previous assignments to Earth, a human habit he understood to be called smoking.

Ripbag was patiently waiting for the opening of the gravity corridor, a space passage which connects the Earth with Polaris, Thurban, Alrai, Aldermin, Vega and Kochab. The gravity corridor opens each lunar month and transports Polestars to and from the intriguing village of Sproatsville in Holderness.

Ripbag had once again been selected by the Star Council of Polaris to visit Earth. The main purpose of his visit was to collect sufficient quantities of Istella, found in abundance in Sproatsville, and transport this much valued resource back to his native star. Istella provides Polestars with their characteristic glow and without this wonder dust they fail to exist. To be chosen for this task was considered an honour, although Ripbag somehow never quite saw it that way, it was more an adventure.

On this occasion however, Ripbag was keen to make the journey because it had been thirty days since he had heard from his best friend, Morgan, who had previously been selected for an assignment to Earth.

All Polestars were aware that failure to return to their home star within the lunar month (twenty nine and a half days) had disastrous consequences leaving them exiled on Earth in a mutant form too ghastly to think about and Ripbag was concerned for the well being and whereabouts of his dear friend.

Everyone in Sproatsville knew about Red Snapper, a beautiful Polestar who suffered the consequence of not returning to her home star before the end of the lunar month. Taking the form of the nearest creature to her before mutation, she now patrols the water around Blue Bell Wood in her deformed state, half Polestar, half fish, terrorising and often devouring innocent Polestars searching for Istella.

Glowing warmly, Ripbag could feel the pull on his body getting stronger and stronger as the gravity corridor began to open. As he waited he purred like a cat with cream, a mannerism peculiar to Polestars. Ripbag loved it when this happened because, contrary to the Code of Practice on Polaris, he would hold onto the nearest boulder, defying the pull until it felt like his pants were about to be torn off his backside. At this point he would let go, to be propelled along the gravity corridor at break neck speed, spinning like a waltzer and screaming with excitement and fear. This was typical Ripbag, always looking for fun and adventure without giving serious consideration to practical things like, 'how am I going to land on my feet when I reach the other end?'

The other end was, of course, Sproatsville on Earth and, on one occasion, whilst performing this ritual, Ripbag had held onto a rock for so long that his pants were actually torn off him and he was transported through the gravity corridor starkers. Luckily, his pants landed on the tip of Three Ways Needle, a landmark situated to the south of Sproatsville and he was able to retrieve them, not though without loss of dignity as the entire incident occurred in full view of Wander, an attractive Polestar who happened to be mining for Istella nearby. To this day, Wander refers to Ripbag as 'Wee Willy' for reasons that probably need no further explanation!

In spite of this, Ripbag managed to pull off a spectacular landing at Windy Gap, an area to the west of Sproatsville. It was called Windy Gap for good reason, it was always windy in this spot and there was a big gap between the nearest village and Sproatsville. Ripbag was not keen on this place, having been previously over-mined for Istella, and it provided little protection and security for Polestars in general.

He soon set about his immediate task to head for Sproatsville and establish contact with other Polestars on assignment to Earth. Being just three and half inches tall, Ripbag was able to cut through fields and hedgerows, which eventually brought him to Gatekeepers Lodge. This was a favourite spot for Ripbag, as the small wooded areas to either side of the lodge were 'chocker' with Istella rocks. His plan was to collect as much as possible early into his visit so as to make time to look for his friend, Morgan.

He began his work without further delay and every so often Ripbag would take one of the small rocks out of his ouzybag, which was used for collecting Istella, crush it into dust and sprinkle the contents down his throat. The reaction was amazing, his whole body began to burst with energy as the dust soaked through his membranes to produce an unbelievable yellow glow all over his body. Ripbag reckoned he had the best glow of all the Polestars but, once again, this was typical Ripbag.

In his haste to commence work, Ripbag had failed to record his arrival in the Assignment Book, the normal practice when Polestars visit Sproatsville. The book was kept under the Grand Old Tree, which stood majestically in the centre of Sproatsville and was overseen by Bullwrinkle, a wise old Polestar, who could recount more stories than a block of flats. Just as Ripbag realised his breach of procedure, he heard a crack that sounded like someone standing on a small branch. Ripbag's glow immediately dimmed, rendering him invisible to the human eye. This was a natural part of a Polestar's defence mechanism and one of the reasons why there had been few sightings by humans. This trick however did not work with

Frombrasent Welps, their sworn enemies, or the ominous and formidable Red Snapper.

Ripbag hardly dare move. Not only had he failed to let anyone know he had arrived in Sproatsville, he suddenly realised that he was in an area frequented by Red herself. The mere thought of her name was enough to dim the glow of a Polestar for eternity, but to feel you're about to make her acquaintance in person was a real glow stopper!

Ripbag was rooted to the spot.

Every branch, leaf and stone seemed to form the shape of some ghastly creature with distorted ghoulish features waiting to tear him apart and for a moment his imagination began to get the better of him. An equivalent human expression would be to 'fill your pants,' a feat Ripbag almost achieved as a hand fell heavily upon his shoulder.

'How yer doing buddy?' a voice boomed.

Ripbag spun on his heels and to his relief, encountered a tall, hairy, scraggy Polestar standing in front of him.

'Dork,' Ripbag screamed. Not that this was the chap's name, it was the only expletive Ripbag could summon to describe him at that moment in time. His real name was Ballbeagle and he was from the star, Aldermin.

'Hey, take it easy man, you've gone a funny colour' said Ballbeagle.

Poor Ripbag was in a stooped position with his hands firmly locked onto his knees doing his best to gather himself.   Slowly his glow returned, he rose, glared at Ballbeagle with a look that could kill at ten paces, then they both burst into laughter.   Ripbag and Ballbeagle touched fingertips, a traditional greeting of friendship between Polestars.   A soft warm radiance lit up their hands momentarily until they parted.   The laughter however didn't last long and was followed by an uneasy silence. Ballbeagle knew Morgan was a close friend of Ripbag and the silence spoke volumes.

'Have you heard anything about Morgan?' asked Ripbag.

'Depends who you talk to,' replied Ballbeagle.   'Some say he left Earth and has visited another star before returning home.'

'And others?' asked Ripbag.

'Others say he fell victim to Red Snapper, or was captured by the Frombrasent Welps.'

Ripbag hung his head low.

'What do you think Ballbeagle?   You know Morgan pretty well.'

Ballbeagle seemed taken aback and, for a moment, looked decidedly uncomfortable at the question but as he began to stutter a response, the sound of the flugelhorn droned eerily like the call of a lost ship on a misty night, providing Ballbeagle with the perfect distraction. The flugelhorn was a signal to all Polestars that a meeting was to take place under the Grand Old Tree, the venue for meetings for thousands of years, and its status amongst Polestars bordered on sacred.

'I guess that means Bullwrinkle is here,' said Ripbag.

There was no response from Ballbeagle who, by this time, was hurtling down the road towards the Grand Old Tree. Ballbeagle had not thrown down a challenge to Ripbag but the words 'last one to the tree is a dork,' might as well have been written all over his back. Watching Ballbeagle run usually had two outcomes - firstly, you would be terrified at the sight of this shaggy, hairy creation coming at you with feet splayed at '10 to 2', and secondly you would just wet yourself laughing. But this time neither applied to Ripbag, who set off at warp speed after Ballbeagle, easily overtaking long before the meeting point.

Ripbag was right, as always, Bullwrinkle was chairing the meeting.

'Nice to see you're here,' said Bullwrinkle looking disapprovingly at Ripbag.

'Always a pleasure,' Ripbag replied as he recorded his late arrival in the Assignment Book. At last Ballbeagle arrived at the Grand Old Tree and joined Ripbag and the other Polestars, who were about a hundred strong by this time.

Bullwrinkle was an amazing Polestar with a memory equal to that of an elephant. He was always at meetings of one sort or another and could regurgitate facts, figures and statistics from matters arising at meetings from the previous century. He was thought to be one hundred and seventy years old although no one knew for sure his true age. Tapping his stave on the thick body of the Grand Old Tree, the purring and chatter from the crowd eventually faded. Bullwrinkle coughed to clear his throat and in a deep authoritative voice began, 'Polestars of the universe, greetings, it is indeed a great honour to be here.'

Ballbeagle reckoned these were the first words to come out of Bullwrinkle's mouth the moment he was born, differing from other baby Polestars who usually purred 'Istella'. Bullwrinkle always opened up with this line before getting down to business, however, what followed was usually very polished and impressive.

Bullwrinkle explained that there were three items of critical importance to be discussed at today's meeting, the first being the Cassiopeia, a prestigious event held annually in Sproatsville. All Polestars take part in this event, with the eventual winner being crowned Polestar Prince or Princess. The Prince or Princess will receive their weight in Istella, if they are judged to have collected the largest amount between ten o'clock and midnight on the eve of the Cassiopeia. In addition, and apart from the esteem that goes with such an accolade, the winner receives possibly the greatest prize of all, 'The Auwnwanx'.

A beautiful mystical creature sought by many and owned by few, the Auwnwanx is the giver of life and through its awesome powers can return from death or mutation those who are worthy. For this sorcerous phenomenon to occur, three criteria must be met. Firstly, there has to be an overwhelming wish for this to be achieved by others. Secondly, there has to be proof of 'goodness' in the previous life of the recipient and thirdly, there has to be evidence of a desire that the subject would wish to return to a new life. When the three conditions are met, the Auwnwanx delivers its immortal feat and the wish, goodness and desire are collectively rewarded with new life.

The Auwnwanx was a gift to the Polestars from Iris, the winged Goddess of the Rainbow, who was eternally grateful for the guiding light their stars provide to her as messenger to the Gods of Olympus. On the eleventh blue moon of the Polestar calendar, on the eve of the Cassiopeia, Iris travels to Sproatsville on the cusp of a beautiful rainbow and bequeaths the Auwnwanx with new wondrous powers for which it will serve the Polestar communities. On the last occasion, Iris invested in the Auwnwanx the gift of life, a legacy which has been cherished by the Polestars since its inception. It therefore has iconic status throughout the whole Polestar fraternity and is fiercely protected.

To become the Cassiopeia's Prince or Princess and be presented with the Auwnwanx was an accolade everyone dreamed of. The Auwnwanx is retained for twelve full moons, a total of three hundred and fifty four Earth days, during which its powers may be accessed on three separate occasions only.

The Cassiopeia culminates in a celebration held at Conny Castle and Bullwrinkle was in full flow dictating and confirming the arrangements leading up to this event. His tone however gradually changed from that of an excited pensioner to a cautious, wise old Polestar with a serious message to deliver.

'There are two other matters which I feel must be brought to your attention,' he said. 'Recently, we have heard about the disappearance of a friend and fellow Polestar. I am, of course, referring to Morgan.'

Concern showed on the faces of those present and small groups began to form, each expressing views on his possible whereabouts.

'No word has been heard from Morgan since his arrival in Sproatsville some time ago,' continued Bullwrinkle. 'This is of great concern to all of us here and his family back home.'

Morgan's disappearance is of even greater concern, considering its timing. Bullwrinkle's eyebrows drew together forming a serious frown.

'For years we have been in conflict with the Frombrasent Welps and I have received reports of a craft landing to the east of Holderness. It is my opinion that the Welps are here to prevent our harvesting of Istella and to unleash death and destruction amongst us. We must remain vigilant at all times and defend ourselves against this evil. Also, we owe it to Morgan to establish a scouting party to determine his whereabouts.'

Bullwrinkle turned tentatively to face Ripbag, showing his longevity and advanced years.

'I sincerely hope Morgan is in the hands of the Frombrasent Welps, however unpalatable that may be,' he whispered. Ripbag understood the context in which Bullwrinkle's otherwise ludicrous comment was made. Suffering the same fate as Red Snapper was unthinkable.

Chapter Two

'Volunteers for the scouting party please raise your hands,' said Bullwrinkle.

Without hesitation, Ripbag raised his hand and at the same time he scanned the remaining Polestars to see who else would accompany him. He knew this wouldn't be an easy recruitment as those who volunteered would have to venture into Bluebell Wood, the domain of Red Snapper and no Polestar in their right mind would want to do that.

Ballbeagle too had volunteered and towards the back of the gathering another hand was raised, although Ripbag couldn't make out who it was. Suddenly a gap opened in the crowd to reveal the third volunteer. It was none other than Jacadaro. Ripbag turned his gaze towards the stars.

'Well, well,' said Jacadaro. 'It looks like we're going to be scouting buddies eh, Ripbag.'

There had always been a bit of history with Jacadaro and Ripbag. Jac was from Kochab and was cool, cute, wore all the latest gear and got right up Ripbag's nose. It didn't help either that Jacadaro was always hanging around Wander, to whom Ripbag was secretly attracted.

Through gritted teeth, Ripbag replied, 'Nice to have you on board, Jac.'

Three was in fact a good number, not too small and not too large to manage, although Ripbag knew in reality that Ballbeagle was not an ideal volunteer due to his lack of speed and agility. There were few Polestars who could match Ripbag and Jacadaro for speed, however, there was another who could leave them both standing and his name was Smirnoff.

Apart from his speed, Smirnoff knew the geography of Blue Bell Wood like the back of his hand, being his favourite mining area before Red moved in. But he had not been near the place since. There was however a slight hurdle to overcome, as Smirnoff had not volunteered, he was scared of his own shadow and was pessimistic about anything and everything. Ripbag's task therefore would be to let Ballbeagle down gently and to find a reason why Smirnoff couldn't refuse. The former turned out to be easy.

Approaching Ballbeagle Ripbag began, 'You know the scouting party that you have just volunteered for?'

'Yes,' replied Ballbeagle.

'Well, you can't go!'

'I know,' said Ballbeagle. 'But I looked pretty cool volunteering didn't I?'

Ripbag just smiled. 'I need to get Smirnoff on board, but I'm not sure how to.'

'Smirnoff!' shrieked Ballbeagle.

'Yes, Smirnoff, don't suppose you've got anything on him have you?'

'But of course,' replied Ballbeagle somewhat hesitantly. 'But of course.'

That evening, Ripbag visited Copper's Corner where Smirnoff lived whilst on assignment. Copper's Corner was actually an old courtroom in Sproatsville and Smirnoff resided under the side entrance in a hole, which led through to the old courtroom chamber. From this small hole, Smirnoff could access any part of Copper's Corner.

Ripbag popped his head through the small entrance and promptly hit it on a sign that read 'Visitors Unwelcome'. He squeezed through further, only to bang his head again on another sign that read 'Dogs Loose'. Ripbag wasn't having any of it. What a miserable toad he thought.

'Smirnoff!' he shouted. 'I know you're here, it's Ripbag, I just want to talk to you. Come on, don't play games, show yourself!'

Ripbag had no sooner got his last word out, when what can only be described as a blur fizzed past his face. Smirnoff was legging it, but unfortunately he miscalculated the hole in the wall and rebounded straight back into Ripbag's arms.

Kicking like a mule, Smirnoff screamed, 'Ain't doing it, ain't doing it, not me, no way. Can't remember anything about Blue Bell Wood!'

'Hey, calm down,' said Ripbag. 'Nobody's going to make you do something you don't want to do.'

'Then why are you here?' asked Smirnoff.

'We just need your help,' replied Ripbag and slowly he released his grip on Smirnoff's collar.

'I hate Mondays,' said Smirnoff.

Ripbag looked bemused. 'Why?' he asked.

'Because Tuesdays follow and I hate them even more!' Smirnoff really was a harbinger of gloom and doom, always seeing the negative in everything. Despite this, Ripbag came straight to the point.

'You've heard about Morgan and you know of the concern shared by all Polestars in Sproatsville and his family. We have an obligation, no..... a responsibility, to determine his whereabouts, however threatening that may be. You know Blue Bell Wood like the back of your hand and the domain of Red Snapper. We simply need to visit the area.'

'Well, why didn't you say that in the first place?' said Smirnoff. 'You can definitely count me out.'

Ripbag stared intensely at Smirnoff, 'Fine, like I said, no one can make you volunteer your services and I'm sure Jacadaro will be most disappointed.'

'Jacadaro,' said Smirnoff. 'Disappointed, what do you mean by that?'

'Well, who wouldn't be disappointed just losing out on being crowned Polestar Prince last year, especially when part of your Istella stash was nicked before the weigh in.'

Smirnoff looked at Ripbag in horror.

Last year, due to a poor harvest, Smirnoff dare not return to Alrai, his star, empty-handed and in sheer panic stole two ouzybags crammed full of Istella from Jacadaro. This left Jacadaro short when it came to the weighing of Istella on the Scales of Justice on the eve of Cassiopeia and subsequently robbed him of the prestigious title, Polestar Prince. Unfortunately for Smirnoff, Ballbeagle witnessed his act of dishonesty but had remained tight-lipped about it, until now. Jacadaro would hang him out to dry if he found out about it.

'Where do we meet?' said Smirnoff, wearing a very dim orange glow.

'We meet at Gatekeepers Lodge at six o'clock tomorrow, don't be late,' said Ripbag.

'Oh, I can't wait,' replied Smirnoff reluctantly.

The next morning Ripbag set about his daily task of collecting Istella. Although his mind was on Morgan and the forthcoming scouting party, he knew how important it was to return to his home star with a good harvest of Istella to please the ruling Council of Polaris.

He decided to mine near a little cottage called Isnthalovely which is reached by a small snicket to the rear of Sproatsville's graveyard. This area always produced a good yield, although there was another motive behind his decision, a little Polestar from Vega called Wander who lived at Isnthalovely during assignment on Earth.

Ripbag soon reached his destination and set about his work picking out lumps of Istella and crushing it into a fine dust. It was a warm clear day and in a short period of time Ripbag had accumulated a decent weight in his ouzybag. It was tiring work so he decided to take a break and enjoy a little of the Istella he had collected. Before doing so Ripbag propped himself up against a tree and opened a dispenser containing water. He was just about to pour this over his head to cool himself down when a little voice whispered in his ear.

'Well, if it isn't Wee Willy Ripbag.'

Ripbag jumped out of his skin, missed his head completely and the water poured all over the front of his pants. Wander burst out laughing.

'Oh, why don't you go for a wander, Wander,' said Ripbag sarcastically.

'Touchy, touchy,' replied Wander. 'Actually, we've just come back.'

'We?' questioned Ripbag.

'Yes, we,' said Jacadaro as he appeared beside Wander. 'Something you could have done with, by the look of your pants!'

Ripbag didn't respond to Jacadaro's wit and simply changed the subject.

'We meet at Gatekeepers Lodge at six o'clock tonight. Smirnoff will be with us too.'

'Smirnoff,' Jacadaro began to laugh. 'It will be dark enough already without his presence and personality.'

'We need him,' said Ripbag, as he turned on his heels to head back to the centre of the village, feeling somewhat humiliated. 'Don't be late!'

'It's a date,' replied Jac, combing his hair and dragging his fringe into the most outrageous peak.

All three Polestars arrived at Gatekeepers Lodge. Ripbag looked focused, Smirnoff very anxious and Jacadaro a million dollars. Ripbag thought Jac could have been going on an intergalactic rave rather than a scouting mission, but there again he never did anything without style. There was no customary touching of fingertips between any of them. Truth be known, none of them would have chosen to be in each other's company.

They soon began their journey to Blue Bell Wood heading down the long narrow road through the Arboretum towards the entrance at Garrison Toll Arch. Trees stood at opposite sides of the roadway, perfectly placed, appearing to form a guard from one end to the other. Whilst beautiful, in the breeze of the night, they swayed gently if not ominously creating a feeling of apprehension and uncertainty.

They were silent as they strolled along in single file, Jacadaro leading, Smirnoff close behind and Ripbag following at the rear just in case Smirnoff tried to leg it!

As they approached Garrison Toll Arch, Smirnoff suddenly grabbed the other two and pulled them off to the side. He explained, to carry on through the arch was not advisable, it was too open and the trees to the right would provide much needed cover. Smirnoff's voice was shaky and faint and if Ripbag and Jacadaro were being honest, they too were very apprehensive about what might lie ahead.

Notwithstanding this, all three moved stealthily forward through the undergrowth, which led to the clearing known as Blue Bell Wood. Smirnoff pointed his finger and whispered to his colleagues, 'It's there, over there.'

Smirnoff was pointing to an area overrun with a blaze of bluebell flowers, which gently sloped down to the edge of the lake. It was picturesque, the sort of scene printed on postcards or reproduced on canvas, hardly the home of a mutant monster. Nevertheless, in spite of its beauty, they all knew they were in the middle of Red Snapper's lair, which sent a chill running from the top of their heads to the soles of their tiny feet.

'Right then,' said Smirnoff. 'I've done my bit, I'm off.'

'Not so fast,' said Ripbag grabbing his collar. 'We came as three and we leave as three.'

Smirnoff knew by the tone in Ripbag's voice that it was pointless arguing so he didn't, he just returned his worried gaze to the scene in front of him wondering what part he was going to play.

Jacadaro suggested that Ripbag and Smirnoff search the area directly in front of them for any evidence of Morgan whilst he circled the back of Blue Bell Wood via Calamity Bridge where they would meet up. If anyone found anything or needed help, they should sound the flugelhorn. All agreed and set about their tasks.

Crawling through the undergrowth of Blue Bell Wood, Ripbag and Smirnoff eventually found themselves in a clearing that led to the water's edge. There were so many nooks and crannies to search they really didn't know where to start for each and every one posed a potentially dangerous and perilous threat.

Smirnoff's keen eyesight suddenly drew his attention to a partially hidden wooden hut on a small island on the lake. He was quick to tell Ripbag of his discovery. Wasting no time, Ripbag began to gather branches and reeds to make a raft. He was anxious to investigate whether the hut on the island would hold clues to his friend's whereabouts. It could not be overlooked.

Meanwhile, Jacadaro was making his way around the back of Blue Bell Wood without getting too close to the lake. He was all too aware of Red Snapper's ability to strike at lightning speed out of the water with devastating effect.

Although in danger of ambush, Jacadaro's journey was quite uneventful and he wondered what his colleagues Ripbag and Smirnoff were up to. The flugelhorn had remained silent so he assumed that they had nothing worth reporting. Little did he know that Ripbag was floating on a raft in the middle of the lake and heading for the hut Smirnoff had sighted earlier.

Ripbag gingerly approached the hut, trying desperately not to disturb the water too much with the large leaf he was using for an oar. Eventually his tiny raft drew up to the edge of the island causing silt and debris to rise all around him.

The over hanging trees dripped moisture relentlessly from the mist, which curiously seemed to hang over the tiny island raising Ripbag's sense of isolation even further.

This was no time to lose your nerve he kept telling himself as he pulled his tiny frame between the long, sharp reeds that pierced themselves menacingly through a carpet of delicate bluebells. His glow was nothing but a dim flicker and his body felt like it was about to implode with every movement that brought him closer to his destination.

In spite of this, Ripbag continued his journey until he was within arm's reach of the door. Cautiously he pushed his head into the gap to peer inside and with relief, yet dismay, discovered it was empty although the floor was covered in very large bird feathers.

As his eyes became accustomed to the dark and damp environment, Ripbag noticed something glistening in the far corner of the hut and retrieved the object for closer inspection. To his horror, he realised he was holding a pendant that had belonged to Morgan.

The pendant had been a gift from Ripbag to celebrate Morgan's first assignment to Sproatsville two years earlier.

Ripbag's worst fears had been confirmed. Morgan must have been captured by Red Snapper and held against his will. There was no other explanation for his pendant being in the hut.

Hastily, he headed back across the lake to join Smirnoff who had been waiting for him. All the fears and insecurities he had experienced earlier had somehow disappeared and were replaced with feelings of helplessness and despair for his best friend, Morgan.

Arriving back, Ripbag quickly shared his discovery with Smirnoff and both set off to find Jacadaro to inform him of their findings.

Looking like he was about to go clubbing, Jacadaro had just started crossing Calamity Bridge to meet up with his friends at the back of Blue Bell Wood as arranged, when he suddenly heard what sounded like singing.

Jacadaro crept slowly to the brow of the bridge, peered over to the other side and to his astonishment saw the cutest little Polestar collecting Istella and putting it in her ouzybag. She had the sweetest of voices and was absolutely stunning. Jacadaro guessed it must be her first assignment to Sproatsville because he had not seen her before and he was familiar with all the female Polestars in Sproatsville. He also surmised she wouldn't be mining in Red Snapper country if she was experienced.

Brushing himself down, Jacadaro peaked his hair and swaggered coolly towards the young Polestar. Momentarily he had forgotten about the purpose of his visit to Blue Bell Wood or the threat posed by Red Snapper and was about to enter 'chat up mode.'

Resting his elbow on the bridge wall, Jacadaro charmingly began, 'Good evening.'

The little Polestar sprang back in surprise.

'My name is Jacadaro, but my friends call me Jac, may I ask your name?'

The little Polestar didn't respond and glared straight at him with the most amazing eyes, vividly beautiful yet dark and intense.

Jacadaro was on a roll and at the beginning of a repertoire of one-liners that just had to be admired, he was as smooth as silk. The little Polestar didn't respond verbally but purred overtly displaying all the behaviours of a young flirtatious female, which encouraged Jacadaro even more.

He couldn't believe his luck and Ripbag couldn't believe his eyes as he caught sight of Jac for the first time since they split. Even on a scouting mission in the back of beyond, Jacadaro had managed to pull whilst standing on the brow of a bridge with the moon silhouetted behind him. Ripbag didn't know whether to feel angry at Jacadaro's disrespect for the group's overall safety or jealousy at his success with the opposite sex, and both he and Smirnoff just stood open-mouthed.

'So, like I said, my name is Jac,' repeated Jacadaro 'And you are?'

'Me?' said the little Polestar, 'I'm, I'm, I'm going to eat you!'

What followed next could only be described as utterly grotesque, as this beautiful little creature grew into a form which towered over Jacadaro, sporting the head of a giant pike with an enormous dorsal fin and the deformed legs and arms of a Polestar.

It was Red, Red Snapper who had the ability to transform herself into the beautiful Polestar she once was, albeit for a short period of time. How foolish could Jac be?

Ripbag and Smirnoff had also witnessed the arrival of Red Snapper and in a moment of madness poor Smirnoff screamed out aloud, 'We're all going to die!'

Turning on his heel, he began his exit from Blue Bell Wood leaving Ripbag enveloped in a cloud of dust. His cowardly retreat caught Red's attention just before she was about to devour Jacadaro. She couldn't believe her luck, two more Polestars and, like a dog that saw a bigger bone, she immediately dived from the top of the bridge into the water, leaving Jacadaro stunned and shaken on the ground. On land Red Snapper was slow and cumbersome but in the water she was awesome.

Fortunately for Jacadaro and Ripbag, Red Snapper was unaware that Smirnoff was also as quick as lightning. However, with a giant pike after his backside he almost became a blur.

Smirnoff's screams could still be heard as he passed Gatekeepers Lodge half a mile away, which was a good indication that Red hadn't even got close to him. Unknowingly, Smirnoff had created the perfect foil for Jacadaro and Ripbag to make their escape through the back of Conny Castle. In reality, Smirnoff had saved Jacadaro's life.

Chapter Three

Ripbag and Jacadaro said little to one another as they made their way back to Sproatsville, partly through their brush with Red Snapper and partly through their sorrow at discovering Morgan's pendant which was now safely tucked away in Ripbag's ouzybag. Neither of them knew what had become of Morgan, however, the signs were not good.

Once they reached Sproatsville they both went their separate ways, Ripbag to the Crooked Cottage, opposite the Grand Old Tree where he lived whilst on assignment and Jacadaro to the Witches Hat, the highest point on top of Sproatsville village hall.

The following morning, Ripbag set out to update Bullwrinkle on their findings from the scouting mission and to tell him of their encounter with Red Snapper.

Bullwrinkle lived in the Church Tower of St Swithun and could often be seen peering out of the small opening just below the large clock. Bullwrinkle's abode was rather fitting for such a grand old Polestar, although it was a bind when it came to visiting him. However, it made him feel king of the castle and no one would disagree he deserved such status.

Ripbag needed some thinking time before meeting Bullwrinkle and decided to take a longer route to the Church Tower through Boggle Lane, which would eventually take him down Lovers Walk and past Isnthalovely Cottage.

He turned down Boggle Lane on auto pilot, lost in his thoughts, and it wasn't until he was opposite Swampy, an unwelcoming water logged wooded area, that his sensibility was awoken by the sound of voices.

Ripbag focused his attention towards the end of Boggle Lane from where the dulcet tones came and couldn't believe what he saw. It was the Frombrasent Welps.

Running for cover, Ripbag dived head first into Swampy, but his landing didn't go with a splash, more a thud, followed by a deep groan, which seemed to come from beneath him.

Almost immediately Ripbag felt himself rising out of the swamp and being flung from the back of the most unsightly creature he had met since Red Snapper. It was 'orrible,' standing tall with mud dripping from a mass of hair. It must be the Swamp Monster, thought Ripbag, although he had never heard of such a creature in Sproatsville.

He didn't know whether to run, hide or feed it! Slowly the monster raised its hands to its eyes and wiped away the sludge to reveal two big white circles.

'How yer doing buddy?' said the monster.

Astonishingly Ripbag replied 'I'm very well, thank you.'

Followed very quickly by 'dork,' as he realised the Swamp Monster was none other than Ballbeagle, his friend.

'Is it your ambition in life to remove the glow from my face forever?' exclaimed Ripbag. 'Whatever possessed you to lie face down in a swamp?'

'It could have something to do with six Frombrasent Welps,' replied Ballbeagle.

'Oh, so you've seen them too?'

'Yes,' said Ballbeagle. 'Err, I was just making my way to the mining fields outside Isnthalovely when I came across them. And the bad news is that Bolo is with them.'

Now, bumping into a group of Welps is bad news for any Polestar, but bumping into one led by Bolo is just simply not clever. He was big, powerful, ruthless and without mercy. Bullwrinkle must have been right when he said a Welp craft had been sighted to the east of the Holderness coast, only now they were here in Sproatsville.

'But why was Bolo here?' whispered Ripbag.

Ballbeagle remained tight-lipped, perhaps due to his fear of attracting their attention. Instead he joined Ripbag peering over a mound of sludge, both looking quite terrifying themselves, as they watched the Welps head out of Sproatsville to return to their craft.

Cautiously, Ripbag and Ballbeagle made their way to the end of the lane to check that the Welps had moved on before turning left towards Lovers Walk and then on past Isnthalovely to Bullwrinkle's home in Swithun's Tower. Bullwrinkle was pleased to see them both, but not to receive the news they had brought him.

'This is terrible,' said Bullwrinkle. 'Morgan was a wonderful Polestar, one can't imagine what has become of him and to hear the Frombrasent Welps are in Sproatsville. Well, this is intolerable, we must act straight away. Ballbeagle, sound the flugelhorn.'

Without hesitation, Ballbeagle grabbed the horn which hung on the wall of the Church Tower, pushed it through the opening below the clock, took a deep breath and blasted out a note which could be heard the length and breadth of the village.

He'd always wanted to do this and suddenly realised why Bullwrinkle seemed to enjoy it so.

It gave you a feeling of power and authority, which secretly Ballbeagle enjoyed.

Moments later, Bullwrinkle, Ripbag and Ballbeagle made their way to the Grand Old Tree where a large number of Polestars had gathered.

Bullwrinkle immediately took centre stage and in his usual commanding style began, 'Polestars of the universe, it is indeed a great honour to be.....' but suddenly stopped short of finishing his usual opening address. After a minor pause, he continued, 'Actually, on this occasion it's not such an honour for I come bearing news of grave concern to us all. It is with great sadness that the scouting party sent out to establish the whereabouts of Morgan discovered his personal pendant in an outbuilding deep inside Red Snapper's domain. We must assume that he is either dead or has suffered the same terrible fate of Red Snapper herself and transformed into a mutant form. If this is true, we dare not contemplate what he has become. Furthermore, it has been confirmed that the Frombrasent Welps are here in Sproatsville.'

Silence befell the crowd as Bullwrinkle continued, 'A division of Welps were seen on the outskirts of the village and it is understood that Bolo was amongst them.'

A wave of panic surged through the crowd at the mention of Bolo's name and Bullwrinkle was all too aware of this.

'Be calm, be calm,' urged Bullwrinkle. 'We are many fold and they are small in number. For the time being, we will work in groups and not alone. I know not the purpose of their visit, but I do know this, the harvesting of Istella will not stop because of their presence. Without it, we cease to exist and no one is going to interfere with the evolution of our race.'

'Here, here,' cheered a small group of Polestars and gradually a warmer glow began to return to their faces.

'And I'll tell you this much,' continued Bullwrinkle. 'The greatest event in the universe is due to take place at Conny Castle soon. I am of course referring to the Cassiopeia.' A loud cheer rose from the crowd. 'It will be the greatest of all celebrations, rewarding the winner with Istella and the bestowal of the sacred Auwnwanx, and nobody, not even Bolo, will interfere with that.'

Bullwrinkle's mention of the Cassiopeia had succeeded in turning the meeting around from doom and gloom to thoughts of 'bring on the marching band.' One had to admire his ability to deliver messages of concern and still leave his audience dancing in the street.

Notwithstanding this, every Polestar knew they had to be on their guard over the coming weeks until their assignments came to an end. It would indeed be an anxious and tense time.

The days leading up to the Cassiopeia were uneventful in comparison with preceding events. Polestars were generally going about their business, some leaving before the great event, others arriving to commence new assignments at such a thrilling time. After what seemed an eternity to some, the Cassiopeia finally arrived and a deep sense of excitement filled the air.

Hundreds of Polestars had congregated under the Grand Old Tree and the atmosphere was electric, not to speak of the glow emanating from such a gathering. The Polestars just looked great and each of them had extra ouzybags strapped to their waists.

Jacadaro, as usual, looked like he'd fallen out of a shop window, Wander was as cute as a kitten, Ballbeagle spaced out, Smirnoff slightly better than miserable and Ripbag focused and determined.

But the star of the show had to be Bullwrinkle. Due to his age, he didn't take part in the Cassiopeia, but instead played the part of Master of Ceremonies. For some unknown reason, he dressed in an amazing gown for these occasions which, when fully robed, made him look like a luminous version of the Earth's Pope, and he loved it.

'Polestars of the Universe, greetings, it is indeed a great honour to be here,' said Bullwrinkle. 'Tonight, I bring you Cassiopeia'.

The crowd screamed with delight.

'By midnight we will have a new Polestar Prince or Princess worthy of their weight in Istella and in recognition of their achievement will inherit the gift of the Auwnwanx.'

Again the crowd roared its approval and Ballbeagle's vacant expression suddenly became very focused at what was going on around him. Not that this was unusual, everyone got excited about the Auwnwanx and Ballbeagle was no different, even if he was considered an outsider for Polestar Prince.

'Proceedings will commence at ten o'clock and will finish upon Swithun's chime at midnight. Polestars will be required to deliver their ouzybags to the weigh-in on the Scales of Justice at Copper's Corner no later than five minutes past midnight or will be disqualified,' announced Bullwrinkle.

'From here, the winner will be carried shoulder high down the back road to Conny Castle, where the celebration and ceremony will begin. May the best Polestar win,' said Bullwrinkle and, without further delay he gave a blast on the flugelhorn to signal the start of the Cassiopeia.

Polestars ran in all directions each hoping to find a spot where a good weight of Istella could be harvested before midnight. The scene bore a striking resemblance to that of a kaleidoscope turning with bright lights exploding from the centre to the outer edges. Happy Polestars clearly were an amazing sight to see.

All too soon for some, Swithun's chime struck midnight and the harvesting was over. Polestars began to make their way to the Scales of Justice at Copper's Corner, some looking smug and pleased with their haul and others the image of disappointment.

One by one the ouzybags were placed on the Scales of Justice to determine their weight and this was recorded along with the Polestar's name by Bullwrinkle.

Jacadaro had done tremendously well with a harvest of twenty grams and had become the target to beat. His nearest rival was Wander and although she wouldn't become Polestar Princess she was taking great delight in beating both Ballbeagle and Smirnoff.

Ripbag was at the back of the queue and had only just made the deadline. As he made his way to the scales, it was obvious that he too had acquired a good harvest, with many ouzybags fit to burst.

The crowd fell silent as he unloaded his cache onto the scales, with both Jacadaro and Bullwrinkle on either side. Ripbag had just one more bag to unload and all would rest upon its contents. He closed his eyes and slowly poured the bag onto the scales. The silence was deafening until Bullwrinkle shouted, 'Twenty two grams, Ripbag weighs in at twenty two grams.'

The crowd erupted and for a brief moment Ripbag wondered why but then he realised that his harvest had beaten Jacadaro by the smallest of measures and he was to become Polestar Prince.

Ripbag performed a dozen somersaults up and down the road outside Copper's Corner and screamed in ecstasy. He just couldn't believe he had become Polestar Prince and in such close circumstances.

Eventually his last somersault landed him back on his feet and just centimetres away from Jacadaro's face.

'I guess I had better offer my congratulations,' said Jacadaro, as he held his hand out somewhat reluctantly. Ripbag knew

Jac was hurting inside but was more concerned about maintaining his cool reputation.

'Thank you,' said Ripbag touching fingertips. 'It couldn't have been closer.'

'A lot closer than last year,' a voice shouted from the crowd.

'Yeah, no Smirnoff around to lighten your load this time Jac.'

Ripbag, being lifted shoulder high, was unaware of these comments and had commenced his journey down the back road towards Conny Castle. Initially Jacadaro didn't respond being somewhat confused, but as he made his way to the celebrations, realisation dawned that his chance of becoming Polestar Prince last year had nothing to do with luck or effort, but everything to do with Smirnoff.

His eyes became narrow and dark and seemed to glisten in the moonlight as he made his way to the greatest event in the Polestar calendar, the Cassiopeia.

Chapter Four

As usual, the Polestars had really gone to town at this year's Cassiopeia. There was music thumping out with dancers skipping around in circles holding hands and this was just at the entrance to the Castle where the Polestar scales awaited the winner.

Ripbag was lifted onto one of the scales, which then became unbalanced, and in turn each Polestar who had taken part in the Cassiopeia threw an ouzybag into the opposite scale until Ripbag drew level. Eventually he balanced nicely with the other side and to his joy he could see the mass of Istella he would be able to take back to Polaris with him.

Ripbag was having a ball. It was a great honour to become Polestar Prince whilst on Earth and he would receive great praise from his ruling Council back home. Chanting his name, the crowd continued the procession to the back of Conny Castle where hundreds of Polestars had gathered.

What an amazing sight, the place looked like it was powered with mini spotlights as the Polestars danced around the huge sacred statues in the grounds. The statues were of past Princes and Princesses and, according to legend, provided protection to those who travelled through the gravity corridor on assignment to Earth. This meant that one day, Ripbag would be cast in stone too.

A large group of Polestars had gathered to take part in a game they called the Big Dipper which was incredibly funny to watch.

A long curved slide resembling a ladle handle had been erected and, at the bottom, a trampoline was in situ. The Polestars launched themselves down the slide and catapulted off the trampoline high onto a separate platform opposite, which was a seat on a pole.

The game had an astronomical relevance as the seat represented Polaris in the constellation 'Little Bear' and the slide and trampoline replicated the Big Dipper, part of the constellation of stars in the 'Great Bear'.

Those who missed the target looked forward to a soft, albeit messy, landing on the other side (a mud tub). Needless to say, few, if any, managed to sit on 'Polaris' and most endured a good dipping.

So the scene was set for a wonderful evening and Ripbag took his place on the throne. The noise generated by the crowd was deafening and for a few moments, Ripbag wondered if he was dreaming.

Reality, however, was confirmed moments later when the crowd parted to reveal Bullwrinkle, with arms raised either side of his head, looking like he was about to conjure up a great surprise.

The crowd fell silent and careful not to lose the moment Bullwrinkle slowly lowered his arms to his side to reveal a truly beautiful, yet awesome sight. It was the Auwnwanx carried by Wander. Tradition demands that the youngest female on assignment presents the Auwnwanx to the winner of the Cassiopeia and Ripbag didn't know where to cast his eyes first. Both the Auwnwanx and Wander had to be the most beautiful things in the Universe.

Purring excitedly, Wander walked towards Ripbag, followed by Bullwrinkle and in turn hundreds of Polestars. Stopping just short of the throne, Wander laid the Auwnwanx on Ripbag's lap and then placed a kiss on his forehead. Ripbag could feel the embarrassment rushing through his body and, just like a human blush, his face turned an even brighter shade of yellow, to the amusement of those close by.

What happened next, however, brought gasps of delight from everyone present. The Auwnwanx came to life, its body bursting with colour, rushing from deep within its mass, exploding onto the surface of the skin. Its impact was both hypnotic and breathtaking.

This wonderful creature had hundreds of gorgeous eyes all individually coloured and with the most outrageous eye lashes. Apart from visual beauty, it also possessed the gift of life and Ripbag was humbled to be able to take the Auwnwanx back to his home star.

All too soon the Auwnwanx returned back to its normal state, leaving everyone in awe of its power and radiance. However none of this meant much to Jacadaro, who had arrived at the Cassiopeia just in time to see the Auwnwanx being presented to Ripbag.

'A wonderful sight, wouldn't you agree?' said Jacadaro who was standing close to Smirnoff. 'All the pomp and ceremony that goes with winning such an event.'

Smirnoff just looked at Jacadaro.

'Some Polestars would give their right arm just to be where Ripbag is right now, don't you think Smirnoff?'

Smirnoff's face lost its entire glow, it was obvious Jacadaro had found out about his dishonesty and in a panic he turned on his heel to escape. But Jacadaro was ready and before Smirnoff could move he grabbed his coat with such force that it almost ripped in two, hanging loosely by his side.

'Some Polestars also lose their right arm for stealing, Smirnoff, what do you think to that?'

'I'll pay it back Jac, I promise I'll pay it back in double, I promise.'

'Oh, I know you will you miserable little oyk, and after that I'm gonna feed you to Red Snapper.'

'Ah yes, of course,' a voice acknowledged from behind the two quarrelsome Polestars.

'Red Snapper, that beautiful little red haired creature that ensnares vulnerable, vain, besotted Polestars before devouring them.' It was Ballbeagle, who had tracked Jacadaro from Copper's Corner.

'Forgive me, Jac,' said Ballbeagle, 'but didn't you have a 'near miss' recently? Rumour has it that if it wasn't for Smirnoff distracting her attention, you would be 'waste matter' at the bottom of Blue Bell Lake by now. Perhaps we shouldn't believe rumour eh, Jac? After all, you wouldn't be treating someone like that if they had saved your life......... would you?'

Jac was staring straight through Smirnoff. He knew Ballbeagle was right and he realised that his loss of Istella and status as Polestar Prince had more than been compensated for. Slowly, he released his grip around Smirnoff's throat dropping him unceremoniously to his knees. An uneasy silence followed before Jac leaned over to Smirnoff and in a soft intimidating tone warned, 'Don't ever bump into me, Smirnoff, not even accidentally, the diplomacy of Ballbeagle will not save you next time.'

Jac rose again and headed off to join the crowd.

'I strongly suggest you heed his advice, Smirnoff' said Ballbeagle, looking somewhat relieved that the colour had returned to Smirnoff's face.

'I will, I will' he replied. 'And thanks for your timely intervention.'

'No need for thanks Smirnoff, just remember who your real friends are. You never know when you might need them, don't you agree?'

Ballbeagle was staring intensely at Smirnoff as if there was a hidden meaning behind his comment, but his expression quickly turned to a big smile, leaving Smirnoff somewhat confused and bemused.

Ballbeagle turned away and began to head towards the centre of the Cassiopeia, turning back momentarily once again to make eye contact with Smirnoff who was following some distance behind.

Celebrations were in full swing and Conny Castle was rocking. Bullwrinkle was right, it was a Cassiopeia to beat all others and Ripbag loved it. Apart from becoming Polestar Prince, Wander was sitting by his side and Jacadaro was nowhere to be seen.

He was just thinking what more could a Polestar want in life when a voice cried out, 'Over there in the sky, look. It's a craft.'

All eyes focused first upon the young Polestar pointing excitedly towards the stars, then to the craft as it grew closer and closer. Gasps came from the crowd as a single battleship, which they knew belonged to their arch enemies the Frombrasent Welps, came into view. The ship was soon hovering above the crowd. They formed a large circle expecting it to land in the middle. As the craft slowly descended Bullwrinkle advised, 'Be calm, remember they are a single force and we are many fold.'

The Polestars had in fact remained calm. They were more curious wondering why a single craft would present itself to such a large gathering.

Although primarily a peaceful and united race, Polestars were very able to defend themselves and most would travel to Sproatsville suitably armed. Their weapons ranged from blade instruments to H.I.T. (High Intensity Thermo) guns which could burn through the most impenetrable defences, causing mass destruction.

However, with light beams punching holes in the dark night and a deep intonation created by the engines, the ship eventually came to land.

All were silent and a sense of uneasiness prevailed. Ripbag remained seated on his throne with Bullwrinkle and Wander either side of him and in front of them the Welps' ship surrounded by hundreds of Polestars.

After what seemed an eternity, the ship's main door hissed, pushing itself out from the smooth contours of the craft's side walls, before descending slowly towards the ground. The light emanating from within the craft was dazzling, so much so that it was difficult to look directly at it. It was only when everyone's eyes adjusted to the intense light that they could see the silhouettes of five Frombrasent Welps standing to attention at the ship's entrance. In unison, their heads bowed and a sixth silhouette appeared. He seemed to take up the whole of the doorway and dwarfed those who had formed the guard. Stopping momentarily to survey the crowd, the huge figure began to walk down the gangway followed by his entourage and it wasn't until he reached the bottom and turned to face Ripbag that everyone suddenly realised who it was.

'Bolo, it's Bolo' whispered the crowd. 'Why is he here?'

He looked awesome, very threatening and distinctly unattractive, although that could be said of all the Frombrasent Welps.

They were an unusual race with a lower body resembling that of a hyena with short legs at the back and long legs at the front which were actually arms. In addition, they had long thick necks which would look more in place on a serpent and when up on their hind legs, which they always were in combat, they looked formidable.

Bolo advanced menacingly towards Ripbag until he was a few yards from the throne. He stopped, turned to face the crowd and said 'Polestars of the universe, greetings, it is indeed a great honour to be here.' Turning back to face Bullwrinkle, Bolo said in a sarcastic tone, 'Oh I'm sorry Bullwrinkle, I do believe that is your line.'

'Quite,' said Bullwrinkle. 'Only your rendition was rather lacking in quality and style.'

'What do you want Bolo?' asked Ripbag.

'Ah, the newly-crowned Polestar Prince and accompanied by a beautiful Princess too,' replied Bolo.

Wander hardly dare look up.

'You haven't answered the question,' said Bullwrinkle. 'You gatecrash our celebrations and place yourself at the hands of hundreds of Polestars, even the mighty Bolo wouldn't be that foolish without cause or reason.'

'Your powers of reasoning never fail to amaze me Bullwrinkle, and once again you are so correct. You see, we have in our possession something we feel is of great value to you. His name is Morgan.'

Ripbag jumped to his feet.

'Morgan!' he exclaimed. 'I don't believe you!'

'Believe what you like' snarled Bolo, as he glared at Ripbag. 'He is with us, in captivity along with others of your race.'

Bolo threw a small package at Ripbag's feet.

'Thought we'd bring you a little something to remind you of him,' said Bolo.

Ripbag bent down to pick up the package which revealed, when opened, a mass of curly golden hair. Only Morgan had such unique hair and they must have shaved his head totally.

'He's alive!' uttered Ripbag to himself. 'He's alive!'

'Yes, for the time being, subject of course to our wellbeing whilst in your company on this wonderful evening,' replied Bolo.

Bolo knew of the loyalty and unity which existed between Polestars and that his safety, and that of his foot soldiers, would be guaranteed in these circumstances.

'So, why are we here?' asked Bolo as he walked around the edge of the circle surrounding him.

'For centuries, both the Welps and Polestars have been sworn enemies and engaged in warfare and conflict. Today, I am here to put an end to such hostilities once and for all.'

Bolo turned swiftly and pointed his finger straight at Bullwrinkle.

'I issue a challenge to you Bullwrinkle, choose your strongest and most feared fighter to meet with me in a duel to the death. The winner takes all, all the wealth, power and authority invested in both our races. There will be no more hostilities, just one victor who will rule the stars between us and, of course, will inherit the greatest prize of all, the Auwnwanx, the giver of life. So what do you say Bullwrinkle, who is courageous enough to take on the mighty Bolo?'

'Sorry to disappoint you Bolo, but I'm not authorised to accept your beastly proposal and, in any event, I'd rather do business with a cobra.'

'Gutless gloworm,' Bolo retorted. 'Perhaps I should just take what I want.'

With that, he snatched the Auwnwanx from Ripbag's lap with his sharp claws and lifted Wander out of her seat. Bolo turned away and stormed towards his ship, his laughter drowning out Wander's screams as a sense of inadequacy and helplessness filled the air at the Cassiopeia. Bolo was just poised to climb the steps of his battleship, when his challenge was unexpectedly met in full.

'I accept,' cried a brave Polestar from within the crowd.

'Who said that? Who accepts my challenge?' said Bolo as he flung both the Auwnwanx and Wander to the ground.

'I do!'

The crowd quickly parted to reveal the unremarkable and dishevelled figure of the brave Polestar who had accepted Bolo's challenge. It was Smirnoff.

'You, you!' exclaimed Bolo, who promptly collapsed into fits of laughter along with his entourage.

'Err, yes, me,' said Smirnoff stuttering his words nervously. 'I won't let you take something that doesn't belong to you, that's wrong.'

'So this is your strongest and most feared warrior Bullwrinkle, ha!' said Bolo.

Bullwrinkle turned to Smirnoff and instructed him to retract his brave acceptance but, before Smirnoff could respond, Bolo threw him a sword from one of his foot soldiers and there was no turning back.

Smirnoff looked at the sword which had landed blade first in the soil. Standing no taller than a human finger, the sword seemed as big as he was. He withdrew it from the ground finding it difficult to control because he was shaking so much.

Both began to circle each other, Bolo on his hind legs and Smirnoff crouching low. Without warning, Bolo lunged at Smirnoff, swinging his mighty sword towards his head but, before he got even halfway, Smirnoff had evaded the attack at lightning speed, leaving Bolo standing. Bolo looked as surprised as he was embarrassed and again launched an attack on Smirnoff, but it was like chasing shadows. In frustration, Bolo screamed, 'Stand and fight me you coward.' He swung his sword again in Smirnoff's direction, only this time Smirnoff side stepped Bolo and landed a slashing blow to his back.

Smirnoff stood in total shock. He couldn't believe he had managed to inflict injury on the mighty Bolo. The crowd gasped, and the whole place fell silent, as blood oozed from the injury.

This sent Bolo into a fury and raising his sword high, he charged at Smirnoff who tried to evade his advance but tripped over his ripped coat as a result of his earlier confrontation with Jacadaro. He fell to the ground, and Bolo towering over him, seized his chance, bringing his sword down with such force that it penetrated Smirnoff's frail, thin body pinning him to the ground. Witnessing his slaughter, the crowd screamed in horror as Bolo's foot soldiers cheered their leader's victory.

Poor Smirnoff had been butchered and lay dying in such terrible circumstances. Ripbag jumped off his throne and ran over to Smirnoff to cradle his head, but it was all too obvious that he was moments from death.

'Why, Smirnoff? Why did you do it? You were no match for Bolo,' Ripbag asked.

Gasping for breath, Smirnoff whispered pitifully, 'It was for Jac, I did it for Jac. I just wanted to make it up to him. Bolo was taking his girl and I wanted to stop him.'

Ripbag's eyes began to fill up.

'You're the bravest Polestar I have ever met, Smirnoff, do you hear me, the bravest by far.'

A half smile crossed Smirnoff's face.

'Will you pass these on to Jac for me, Ripbag?'

Smirnoff produced two small ouzybags from his ripped coat pocket, but before Ripbag could reply, Smirnoff's hand dropped to the ground and he was gone.

'I guess you'll be needing this,' said Bolo, as he dangled the Auwnwanx over Smirnoff's head. 'Pity you don't own it anymore, isn't it. In fact, I don't believe the Polestars own anything anymore, Ripbag.'

'Actually I do,' replied Ripbag. 'I own these.'

Ripbag stood up and slowly drew two plectrones from his back holster. These were traditional Polestar short swords and Ripbag's father was a past master in their use. He had spent many hours schooling Ripbag in armed combat in the event one day he may need to use them, and it seemed that day had arrived.

'At last, a real challenger, the Polestar Prince,' said Bolo. 'I'd offer you a real weapon Ripbag, a Welp's battle sword, only it seems to be stuck in your friend's chest right now!'

Ripbag didn't respond, he simply took a pinch of Istella from one of Smirnoff's ouzybags, tilted his head back and sprinkled the dust onto his tongue. With that, Bolo picked up the sword that Smirnoff had used moments earlier and lunged towards Ripbag, aiming a blow at his head. Ripbag met the sword in a defensive cross and, by using his feet, delivered a blow to

Bolo's chest. Both engaged each other again, attacking and defending ferociously and Bolo's power looked as if it would overwhelm anything that got in its way.

Ripbag needed to recall all his father had taught him and more, to deal with this animal who seemed oblivious that he was dripping with blood from his encounter with Smirnoff. Through determination, courage and skill however, Ripbag was holding his own and as the fight progressed he began to push Bolo back with fierce combinations.

For the first time, Bolo looked perplexed and Ripbag, urged on by the sad sight of Smirnoff's body, found inner strength that he had not experienced before. Bolo was suddenly there to be taken and, seizing his opportunity, Ripbag scythed a blow to the base of Bolo's sword, sending it spinning into the air and out of reach. Filled with aggression, Ripbag moved in to finish Bolo off but just as he was poised to bring both daggers down into his huge frame, one of the Welps foot soldiers intervened, sending Ripbag tumbling to the ground, saving his master from certain death. Bolo ran to retrieve his sword and positioned himself to finish the young Polestar off.

'Be still,' howled Bullwrinkle, pointing his finger at Bolo. 'You are a cheat and without honour and we will not let you leave this land if any harm comes to Ripbag.'

Bullwrinkle had no sooner intervened when the sound of a spinning blade was heard whirling towards him thrown by the same foot soldier that had tripped Ripbag. The blade made a sickening thud as it plunged into the middle of Bullwrinkle's chest, sending this old gracious and respected Polestar to his knees.

'Bullwrinkle!' yelled Ripbag. 'Oh no, what have you done?'

'And now Ripbag, it's time for you to join your two colleagues,' snarled Bolo.

Wander began to scream hysterically at the prospect of the imminent slaughter of the new Polestar Prince, but in truth her screams were directed elsewhere.

Out of the sky descended the most hideous of creatures. It had a massive wing span, the head and claws of a hawk and the torso of a crippled and twisted Polestar and came swooping down poised to pick up prey on the wing. It opened its wide, sharp claws and grabbed Bolo, lifting him high in the air. Bolo screamed in agony as its claws punctured every part of his body, but his screams were drowned by the creature's ear piercing squeal as it hovered above the crowd.

Ripbag lay motionless and bewildered on the ground as the creature lowered itself towards him. For a few moments, it stared at Ripbag, not altering its glare with Bolo hanging like a butchered piece of meat. Ripbag was transfixed and dare not move. It was as if this creature had purposely saved him from the dishonourable blade of Bolo but what was it, who was it? Turning its head, the creature set off high into the sky with Bolo trailing from its talons and immediately the remaining Frombrasent Welps were seized by the angry crowd.

Wander rushed over to Ripbag, followed by countless others concerned for his welfare, but Ripbag was numb. Apart from all that had gone before him, Ripbag was shocked at what he had just seen, probably more so than anyone else.

'It was Morgan,' he whispered.

'Morgan? Come on little fella, let's get you to your feet, no one knows who or what that was,' said Ballbeagle as he watched with a strange sense of concern as the creature disappeared into the distance, prey dangling beneath.

'I know what I saw Ballbeagle, it was Morgan, he is a mutant. My friend has suffered the consequences of overstaying his welcome in Sproatsville, engineered by Red Snapper, may the Gods help him.'

Just at that moment, a voice called out.

'Ripbag, the Auwnwanx, bring it quickly.'

Ripbag suddenly refocused realising that the Auwnwanx had the power to save both Bullwrinkle and Smirnoff. Ripbag raced over to where Smirnoff was lying. The sword so cruelly delivered by Bolo had been removed from his body, which lay pathetically on the ground. The Auwnwanx was placed over Smirnoff and immediately it began to function.

Although Smirnoff was now viewed as a thief, the Auwnwanx had acknowledged the overall good in his life, which was one of the criteria required to receive the benefit of its powers.

The most beautiful colours exploded from deep within its body, covering the whole of Smirnoff and in turn reflected off the faces of those looking on. Slowly, the eyes of this magical creature began to open and almost simultaneously the most amazing glow returned to Smirnoff's face, to the sheer delight of his friends.

'Thank goodness we were in time' said Jacadaro as he watched Smirnoff being encouraged to his feet. His previous anger with Smirnoff had somehow lost its edge after witnessing his encounter with Bolo although Smirnoff was by no means forgiven.

Ripbag immediately went to Bullwrinkle's side and covered his body from head to toe with the Auwnwanx. Once again the response was instantaneous. Bullwrinkle slowly opened his eyes and purred to the cheers of hundreds of Polestars, and in particular, to the relief of Ripbag who always viewed Bullwrinkle with great respect.

'Ah, the Auwnwanx,' said Bullwrinkle in a frail voice. 'I take it you triumphed over Bolo, and Sproatsville is once again a safe place for Polestars to visit?'

'Yes,' said Ripbag.

'Today you became a real hero and a true leader, I am so proud of you Ripbag,' said Bullwrinkle.

'There is no bigger hero than you around these parts Bullwrinkle, and before you know it, we'll have you back on your feet again doing all the things that only Bullwrinkle can do.' Once again, all the eyes of the Auwnwanx suddenly opened and Bullwrinkle gave Ripbag a contented smile.

'I'm an old Polestar now Ripbag and I've seen and done many things in my time. Just like you, I was sent here to represent my star and to harvest Istella but I'm tired Ripbag, so tired, and I question whether I can fulfil my responsibilities or have the energy to do so anymore.'

'What are you talking about Bullwrinkle? Everything's going to be just fine, you'll see,' said Ripbag.

'No, Ripbag, my time has come, it's time to move on.'

There was a noticeable lack of energy coming from the Auwnwanx and its beautiful eyes one by one began to close. Ripbag was aware that there were three conditions that had to be met in order for the Auwnwanx to reward the gift of new life. One, there had to be an overwhelming wish for this to be achieved by others. Two, there had to be evidence of goodness in the previous life and three, there had to be a desire by the individual to return to a new life. Two of the three conditions had been met in their entirety, everyone loved Bullwrinkle, especially Ripbag, and he was the epitome of goodness, an example to all Polestars. However, he had given so much during his life that he had no more to give, and the third condition, a desire to return to a new life, was sadly no longer there.

Ripbag's eyes were brimming with tears.

'Please don't go, Bullwrinkle, please stay with us, we need you.'

Bullwrinkle smiled once again and grasped Ripbag's hand.

'One day, the time will be right for you too and only then will you understand.'

'I love you, Bullwrinkle,' said Ripbag. 'We all love you, we will never forget you.'

Bullwrinkle's eyes turned towards the stars and, drawing his last breath, he whispered pitifully, 'Remember this, Ripbag, '*He who dances with fire will truly receive his greatest desire.*' Until we meet again Ripbag wherever that may be.'

He said no more and the eyes of the Auwnwanx came to a close. Bullwrinkle had passed away.

Chapter Five

A deathly silence fell around the grounds of Conny Castle. Bullwrinkle had promised a Cassiopeia never to be forgotten and once again he had delivered, although no one expected it would be in such distressing circumstances.

Ripbag laid Bullwrinkle's head gently on the ground, brought himself to his feet and turned to face his fellow Polestars. 'The Cassiopeia is over, there will be no more celebrations. Today we have lost a legend amongst Polestars.'

Without instruction or direction, all those present formed a guard of honour, which stretched all the way to the main gates of Conny Castle.

Ripbag, Ballbeagle, Jacadaro and Smirnoff placed Bullwrinkle onto a piece of tree bark as a makeshift stretcher and lifted him to the upward facing hands of the leading Polestars and the process of transporting Bullwrinkle back to Swithun's Tower began. As soon as the stretcher had passed over the Polestar's heads, they would make their way to the front of the guard to ensure that a continuous momentum was maintained until Bullwrinkle reached Swithun's Tower, where he would remain until the next day.

What had started out as a celebration to mark Ripbag's inauguration as Polestar Prince had ended with a procession of mourners in Bullwrinkle's honour and the Cassiopeia had come to a close in an unprecedented and tragic way.

The following day was a low key affair with few Polestars seen out and about. A feeling of despair hung over Sproatsville and Ripbag had spent most of the day preparing for his return to Polaris. His assignment had been filled with adventure, achievement and finally grief and would see him transporting Bullwrinkle back home through the gravity corridor to Thurban and then on to his own star, Polaris. In addition, he couldn't stop thinking about his encounter with Morgan, his close friend, and the fact that he had become a mutant at the hands of Red Snapper. What was he going to say to Morgan's family?

As night began to fall, Ripbag decided he would visit Wander to say goodbye. This was the first time he had ever done so as, in the past, he had always wanted to but felt embarrassed and chickened out when he got to the gate of Isnthalovely.

When he arrived, Wander was sitting at the entrance gazing across the open fields, almost as if she was waiting for him.

'Hello Ripbag,' she said. 'I'm pleased to see you've made it to the gate this time.'

Ripbag was taken aback by her comment as he didn't realise she was aware of his previous failings and he began to blush. Wander sprang to her feet and walked towards Ripbag.

'Nevertheless,' she said. 'I am really pleased you're here, shall we go for a stroll?'

Both Ripbag and Wander headed towards Lover's Walk, a small snicket running between Isnthalovely and the open Istella fields which then led to Boggle Lane. It was the time of the year when the foliage of the overhanging shrubs and bushes down Lover's Walk formed a beautiful tunnel, the end of which was illuminated by the sun at the point of the Kissing Gate.

Lovers Walk was appropriately named and in normal circumstances provided the perfect surroundings for romantic encounters. Not today however, the events of the previous evening put paid to any thoughts of romance either of them may have had.

'I can't believe what happened last night,' said Wander. 'It's almost as if it didn't happen at all, as if it was a dream which I awoke from this morning, but it did happen and it seems so surreal.'

Ripbag was silent.

'Why did Bullwrinkle forego the gift of life? He was loved by everyone, he had so much to offer, so much knowledge and wisdom, it seems such a waste and how courageous of Smirnoff to do what he did, even though he was indebted to Jac. I wonder what will happen to him now? Having committed a crime in Sproatsville the ruling Council of Alrai will not look favourably upon him when he returns.'

'I don't know,' said Ripbag. 'They may send him to Capper, which is an icy cold star where Polestars are punished for their crimes but I don't think his crime justifies that. He may be a miserable toad but he doesn't deserve to join the low lives on the Capper Flow.

'Jacadaro may disagree,' said Wander. 'He was gutted about missing out on becoming Polestar Prince last year.'

'Yes, I can understand that,' said Ripbag. 'You're fond of Jacadaro, aren't you?' enquired Ripbag.

'I like him,' said Wander. 'Oh I know he's a show off, but he's funny too.'

By this time, Ripbag and Wander had reached the end of Lover's Walk and were at the

Kissing Gate. Wander turned to Ripbag and clasped both his hands.

'I thought I was going to,' she faltered. 'I mean, we all were going to lose you last night in the fight with Bolo, you were so brave, Ripbag.'

Unmoved by Wander's praise, Ripbag replied, 'Thank you, but part of me wishes I had been taken by Bolo. Bullwrinkle was like a father to me and my best friend Morgan is living a nightmare forever exiled in Sproatsville. I'm all alone, Wander, so alone.'

Wander didn't get a chance to reply to Ripbag's comments as Ballbeagle suddenly arrived on the scene.

'Well, if it isn't my good friends, Ripbag and Wander.' Ripbag let go of Wander's hands quickly.

'Err, I'm going to have to make tracks,' said Ripbag. 'There is still much to do and I must get to Windy Gap in time for the opening of the gravity corridor.'

'Make sure of that,' said Ballbeagle. 'Wouldn't want anything untoward to happen to you.'

'I will my friend,' Ripbag bid goodbye to Wander and began to make his way down towards Boggle Lane.

'I don't envy him right now,' said Ballbeagle, 'even though he is Polestar Prince. His journey to Thurban will be a long and difficult one and his return to Polaris equally traumatic. What will he say to Morgan's family?'

Wander just shook her head.

'May Iris, the Goddess, protect him on his travels and stay with him,' she replied, as they both walked slowly back towards Isnthalovely.

Making his way down Boggle Lane, Ripbag could have been forgiven for believing that the remainder of his time on assignment would be incident free, but how wrong could he be. Ripbag decided to stop off at Swampy where he had previously taken cover when he came into contact with the Frombrasent Welps. He did this because his boots were covered in mud and dirt from his encounter with Bolo and this was an opportunity to wash away the dirt and hopefully the memory.

Swampy was not the most welcoming of places and some Polestars refused to go there. It always seemed to be dark and cold, even on sunny days, and there was a constant eerie feel which led to a deep sense of insecurity for those who visited the area.

Ripbag didn't intend to stay long, he sat down against the roots of a tree overhanging the swamp and took off his boots, then knelt and leaned over the swamp. Ripbag began to cup water into his hand and scrub his boots until they were almost as good as new. The water, although dirty, was like glass and reflected the terrain around it like a large distorted mirror.

Gazing down in the swamp water, Ripbag could see all above and behind him, clouds, branches, hedgerows and birds, including the head of a massive hawk with piercing eyes glaring down upon him. It took quite a while to register in Ripbag's head that the image of an enormous hawk's head was not really an acceptable part of the surrounding environment and, although his reaction was delayed, he quickly turned around to confirm what he had just seen in the reflection of the water.

Ripbag gasped in disbelief. The creature that had speared Bolo with its huge talons and dragged him off into the night was perched in the tree and looking straight at him with the most evil eyes.

'Morgan,' cried Ripbag, as he pushed himself further away from the tree with his heels. 'It's you, Morgan, isn't it?'

To Ripbag's surprise the creature responded.

'Stay away from me, Ripbag, stay away.'

'But, but I can help you Morgan, let me help you,' stuttered Ripbag.

'My destiny is clear, Ripbag, I'm not the person you knew and never will be again.

Yesterday I chose to save you, tomorrow will be different.'

'But I am the Polestar Prince, Morgan, the Auwnwanx is at my disposal, please let me help you.'

The creature flapped its huge wings, launched itself from the tree branch and hovered above Ripbag's shaking body.

'Stay away, Ripbag, don't ever visit Sproatsville again. Heed my advice, do you hear and don't ever return.'

The creature's claws were wide open as the message was delivered and for a moment Ripbag felt he may suffer the same fate as Bolo, however, the half bird, half Polestar turned and flew off into the distance.

Ripbag jumped to his feet shouting loudly, 'I won't give up on you, Morgan, I'll never desert you, do you hear, never.'

Still shaking from his encounter, Ripbag ran from Swampy and didn't stop until he arrived at his home, the Crooked Cottage. He quickly gathered his personal belongings together, including the Auwnwanx and set off towards Swithun's Tower, where arrangements were in place for Bullwrinkle's body to be transported to Windy Gap.

Upon arrival, Ripbag could see that everything had been immaculately prepared and three fellow Polestars were waiting to accompany him and Bullwrinkle on what would be his final departure from Sproatsville.

It was a sad moment to see Bullwrinkle's body, draped in his favourite robes, being pushed away from Swithun's and hundreds of Polestars gathered on the road to Windy Gap to pay their last respects. It seemed to mark the end of an era but the journey had to begin and so it did.

Windy Gap was of course the place where Ripbag landed when commencing this assignment and in order for Polestars to be transported back through the gravity corridor they needed to return to the same area of entry when it reopened.

Laden with Istella and with the Auwnwanx over his shoulder, Ripbag, with the assistance of his friends, pushed the body of Bullwrinkle on a beautifully decorated dray all the way to the point of departure.

Soon after, he bade farewell to his friends and was left alone contemplating the journey which lay before him. It was a sad sight, only the silhouettes of Ripbag and Bullwrinkle could be seen against the backdrop of a full moon, with Sproatsville twinkling in the distance.

Purring contently but waiting patiently, there would be no more games or fooling around on this occasion, he just wanted to be on his way.

Suddenly, out of the darkness came a voice 'Ripbag, Ripbag,' the voice repeated.

In shock, he jumped to his feet and stared straight at Bullwrinkle. He's talking to me from the other side, thought Ripbag.

'Is that you, Bullwrinkle' he hesitantly enquired.

'No, it's me,' a voice replied, as the figure of a Polestar strode out of the bushes. It was Ballbeagle.

'I know, I know,' said Ballbeagle. 'I'm a dork, but wouldn't life be boring without my little surprises?'

Ballbeagle held out his hand and placed a small envelope in Ripbag's hand.

'Wander asked me to give you this, old friend, before you leave.'

Ripbag opened the beautifully decorated envelope and in the light of the moon read the contents of a small note, which simply said, 'together we will never be alone.'

He smiled briefly, looked at Ballbeagle and said, 'Thanks pal, you're one of the nicest dorks one could ever wish to meet.'

Ripbag and Ballbeagle began to laugh, a sharp contrast to the mood which prevailed before Ballbeagle's arrival. When the laughter stopped, Ripbag focused his eyes on Bullwrinkle's body and asked Ballbeagle, 'What do you think he meant?'

'Say again, my friend?'

'*He who dances with fire will truly receive his greatest desire,*' said Ripbag. 'Those were his last words to me before he died.'

'Err...... Bullwrinkle was a deep and wise old Polestar, Ripbag, and I doubt if we will ever find out the meaning behind his prophecy,' replied Ballbeagle somewhat hesitantly.

Ripbag continued to stare at Bullwrinkle, hoping the longer he did this the clearer things would become, but they didn't. Instead, his body began to shake and his face started to shudder and distort with the pull of gravity.

'Wow, it's time my friend, I can feel it.' Ripbag's body began to glow more intensely as the gravity pull became more evident on his body.

'Stand back, Ballbeagle, and wish me luck.'

'You've got it man,' said Ballbeagle hastily touching fingertips.

'Until the next time,' said Ripbag, as he took hold of Bullwrinkle's hand and, with that, the gravity corridor opened fully and both he and Bullwrinkle were sucked into deep, dark space at scorching speed.

Ripbag's assignment had come to an end, although Ballbeagle sensed, somewhat uncomfortably and for reasons only he knew, that it wouldn't be too long before he returned to Sproatsville once again.

Chapter Six

Life in Sproatsville continued as normal over the coming weeks and months with new Polestars arriving in pursuit of the valuable resource, Istella. Meetings took place under the Grand Old Tree and the procedures and practices, many of which had been established by Bullwrinkle, were continued by other leading Polestars but somehow they lacked influence and quality.

A charismatic dominant figure was desperately needed in Sproatsville to lead by example and to further develop the collective spirit for which Polestars were renowned, but only time would determine who that may be.

Ballbeagle, Jac and Wander had all returned to their respective stars and would only return to Sproatsville on new assignments if requested by their ruling Councils. In reality, however, they could expect to make two or three visits each year. Ballbeagle, for example, had been selected on numerous occasions by his ruling Council to visit Sproatsville in the past year, although one couldn't understand why, as he was not that successful when mining for Istella. Perhaps for other reasons his Council felt he was a good ambassador for his star, Aldermin, and were keen to secure his services.

As for Smirnoff, his luck seemed to go from bad to worse. One day as the gravity corridor opened, not too long after Ripbag's departure, it revealed the ominous figures of two Alrai guardsmen standing side-by-side at Coppers Corner. The guardsmen were the custodians of law and order on Alrai and word had spread about Smirnoff's dishonesty whilst on assignment, an act which would not be tolerated. In shame, but also with some sadness, Smirnoff was taken away to answer for his crime which, as predicted by Ripbag, subsequently resulted in him being sent to Capper by his ruling Council. Smirnoff would now be held on Capper until it was felt he had paid the penalty for his crime.

Unfortunately for most, however, survival on Capper for the average Polestar was nothing more than twelve lunar months, due to the harsh regime, cold atmosphere and rations of Istella. The future looked very bleak for Smirnoff.

As for Morgan, his reputation as a mutant Polestar began to grow and, like Red Snapper, he acquired a degree of notoriety and reverence, which struck fear into the hearts of those making the journey to Sproatsville. Stories of Polestars being ripped apart by the talons of Morgan were rife, if not always true. Most of these were based upon the sudden disappearance of two Polestars, who vanished without trace when on assignment. In reality, anything could have happened to them, bearing in mind the constant threat from the Frombrasent Welps, not to mention Red Snapper, although it seemed Morgan had become the focus of attention and, in fairness, he couldn't be overlooked.

By this time, Ripbag had made the journey to Thurban and had since returned to Polaris. Ripbag was hailed a hero firstly for becoming Polestar Prince and, secondly, for his duel with Bolo that had ultimately led to Bolo's death, albeit via the claws of Morgan. Ripbag, however, took no joy from his celebrity status and had spent much time thinking about and planning his return to Sproatsville. The journey to Thurban had been traumatic for Ripbag, witnessing first hand the despair and grief shared by Bullwrinkle's family and fellow Polestars. He was an icon on Thurban too, as well as in Sproatsville and Ripbag's sense of loss had been magnified and compounded even further.

By the new fourth lunar month in the Polestar calendar, Ripbag had convinced his ruling Council that he should be permitted to return to

Sproatsville on assignment, although he did not explain that his primary purpose was to seek out the mutant, Morgan. Had this been so, it was more likely that authorization to enter the gravity corridor would have been refused.

Armed with ouzybags, various mining tools and other personal items, Ripbag took his place at the highest point on Polaris waiting for the gravity corridor to open. Slung over his shoulder was the greatest gift any Polestar could ever wish to possess, the Auwnwanx, which had been presented to Ripbag at the Cassiopeia.

Ripbag had been careful to hide the Auwnwanx up to this point, as questions would have been asked as to why on this visit he wished to take it to Sproatsville. No such explanation was going to be required, as the pull on Ripbag's body began to grow stronger and stronger. The gravity corridor was opening and, as ever, Ripbag was about to launch himself outrageously into the night against all rules of protocol.

Moments before his departure however, he was unceremoniously joined by a female Polestar, who jumped onto his shoulders before the gravity corridor swept them both off their feet, sending them tumbling through space towards Sproatsville.

Ripbag wondered who this crazy Polestar could be and why she was wrapped around his neck, although this wasn't his prime concern. For once, Ripbag was actually thinking about his landing and how he was going to manage it with this lunatic hanging off him. He need not have worried however, as moments before they were due to make touchdown, the female Polestar sprang from his shoulders, rotated like a Catherine wheel and made a perfect landing on two feet, without a step back or forward. Ripbag, for his part in this fiasco, slid on his backside and was brought to a halt when a large flagpole firmly planted in the middle of a green in Sproatsville split his difference! Lying flat on his back, Ripbag tilted his head to look behind him and saw the face of a young Polestar giggling as she stood over him.

'Oh no, oh no,' shrieked Ripbag. 'Your father will kill you, and me,' he said jumping to his feet. 'Are you crazy? What are you doing here?'

'No, I'm not crazy and I'm here for the same reason you are,' she said.

'You can't be,' said Ripbag. 'You're not old enough to come on assignment.'

'I've not come to collect Istella, Ripbag, and neither have you. I know why you are really here.'

A few moments of silence fell between them.

'I have to be here, Ripbag,' said the young female emotionally. 'Morgan is your best friend, but he is my brother, he needs my help.' Ripbag stepped forward and wrapped his arms around her.

'Of course, I understand, of course I do.'

The youngster's name was Miranda Moon and after brushing himself down, Ripbag decided he would record their arrival in the assignment book. Ripbag was a little concerned about doing this as Miranda was not supposed to be on assignment, but he figured under the circumstances she should be accounted for. Hastily Ripbag set off with Miranda in tow, but managed only a few short steps before a beam of light flashed across the Istella fields laying bare the night moths and fire flies sending field mice scurrying for cover.

Ripbag pushed Miranda into the swaying crop and sank slowly to his knees invisibly safe from the approaching human.

'Who is he?' whispered Miranda.

'That's Mad Pete' replied Ripbag. 'Some years ago, after the Cassiopeia, one of the humans working at Conny Castle reported seeing small folk with glowing bodies dancing in the gardens. He was regrettably relieved of his post on the grounds of insanity, it was Mad Pete. Today he still maintains his belief but only at the ridicule of the locals who believe that large gatherings of fire flies which swarm around the garden statues are a more likely explanation. Mad Pete remains undeterred however and spends much of his time searching the land around Sproatsville. That's why he's known as Mad Pete.'

Snorting like a bull in a field he grew closer and closer.

'Come on show yourself,' he snarled, 'I know you're here.'

Driven by a desire to free his mind and prove his sobriety he stormed past Ripbag and Miranda like a lighthouse on legs, scything his torch beam from side to side.

Ripbag and Miranda's glow soon returned after Mad Pete had passed by and they were clearly visible once again.

'Come on,' said Ripbag. 'We don't want to be hanging around just in case he comes back.' Cautiously they both emerged from the field.

Their ability to become invisible in the presence of humans had ensured their safety, as it had for many Polestars before them. The incident was nevertheless a timely warning to Miranda that visiting Sproatsville, whilst exciting, was a hazardous and dangerous thing to do.

Arriving at the Grand Old Tree, Ripbag noticed that two of his friends were also on assignment once again in Sproatsville. They were Jac and Wander, although it still wasn't clear in Ripbag's mind whether Jac fell into the category of friend. Nevertheless, Ripbag was pleased to see some familiar names and would need their help in what was about to unfold in the coming days.

The following morning, Ripbag and Miranda Moon emerged from the gap in the step at Crooked Cottage and headed towards Isnthalovely. The intention was to mine for Istella in that area but also, if Ripbag was being honest, to make his acquaintance with Wander.

Soon after turning down the little snicket at the back of Swithun's Tower, Ripbag and Miranda bumped into Jacadaro. Miranda had never met Jac before and was immediately taken in by this cool character with a silky tongue. On this occasion, however, Jac was not his usual smooth self and, in fact, was rather subdued. He was all too aware of the difficult time Ripbag had been through recently and was showing compassion and respect, instead of his usual sarcastic wit.

'How's things?' asked Jac. 'I understand your trip to Thurban was not easy?'

'No,' said Ripbag.   'It will remain with me forever.'

'I wish I could have done something to help,' said Jac. 'If I hadn't been so preoccupied with Smirnoff I may have been able to prevent that foot soldier throwing his.......'

'No,' Ripbag interrupted.   'It was not your fault.'

Jac's head hung low and Ripbag was taken aback by his assumed guilt.

'Bullwrinkle's death was not of your doing and in any event he chose his own destiny and we have to respect that.'

Jac nodded his head and slowly raised his eyes until they locked on to Miranda.

Purr, purr.....'Why, you've forgotten your manners, Ripbag.   Who is this beautiful creature?' Purr...........

Ripbag wondered how long it would be before Jac became his normal self.

'My name is Miranda Moon,' said the young Polestar innocently offering her hand.

'Miranda Moon, what a wonderful name, quite unforgettable.'

Jacadaro's fingertips made contact with Miranda and remained there for quite some time. Ripbag coughed in annoyance.

'She's also known as Morgan's sister,' said Ripbag.

Jacadaro withdrew his hand immediately and, for the second time in as many minutes, looked decidedly uncomfortable.

'Oh really,' he said. 'Oh right, well I'd better be making tracks then, err, I'm very pleased to have met you, Miranda Moon, I'm sure we'll meet again.'

'Tonight soon enough for you Jac?' asked Ripbag.

'Tonight?' repeated Jac.

'Yes, tonight, I want to discuss something with you and Wander, it's important, shall we say eight o'clock at my place?'

'The pleasure is all mine,' said Jac, as he regained his composure. 'It's a date,' he said staring directly at Miranda, who then began to blush a brighter shade of yellow.

Ripbag looked disapprovingly at Miranda, as her colour began to return to normal.

'He's not to be trusted,' said Ripbag as he strode off towards Isnthalovely. 'You would do well to remember that.'

Miranda didn't respond and fell in line behind Ripbag until they reached the mining fields opposite the beautiful little cottage where Wander lived.

'Who is Wander?' asked Miranda, 'I've heard you mention her name before.'

'Err, she's just a good friend,' said Ripbag staring nervously at the entrance gate.

'Ain't you gonna call on her?'

'Highly unlikely,' a voice replied from behind the hedge. It was Wander, looking a million dollars.

'You see, he seems to have a fear of gates, especially when it comes to opening and walking through them. Isn't that so, Wee Willie?'

'Wee who?' asked Miranda.

'Err, never mind that,' said Ripbag. 'Wander, I'd like to introduce you to Miranda Moon, Miranda is....'

'Morgan's sister,' interrupted Wander.

'Oh, so you know then?'

'Well, apart from the likeness, Morgan had told me all about his pretty sister and her extraordinary skills as a gymnast. Why, you can practically fly according to him. Morgan was very proud of you,' said Wander.

'I know and I intend for him to remain so,' replied Miranda.

Wander looked inquisitively at Ripbag.

'All will become clear tonight, Wander,' he said. 'Will you come to see me at eight o'clock?'

'Well, Ripbag, that's the best offer I've had in ages. Of course I will.'

'Great, we look forward to seeing you.'

By this time, Miranda had begun to explore the fields outside Isnthalovely. She had never seen so much Istella and was instinctively beginning to collect small amounts to take back to Polaris. Ripbag took advantage of this private moment.

'I'm so pleased you're here, it was great to see your name in the assignment book.'

Wander smiled, 'I guessed you would be back around this time, although I have to say unaccompanied.'

'I had little choice in the matter,' said Ripbag. 'Her father will be aware by now as well, he'll go spare.'

'Oh, what a complex life you lead,' said Wander. 'Never a dull moment.'

'Most of it, not of my making,' replied Ripbag.

Miranda had continued to collect Istella whilst Ripbag and Wander talked and by now was glowing as brightly as her name might suggest. She had ingested most of the Istella, instead of collecting it.

'Boy, this is brilliant,' she said. 'I can't wait 'til I am old enough to come on assignment.'

'Your time will come soon enough,' said Ripbag, who couldn't help but chuckle at her appearance.

'So, eight o'clock then Wander, at my place.'

'I'll be there Ripbag, I'll be there.' She then recommenced her harvesting.

Ripbag and Miranda continued their journey on through Lovers Walk and into Boggle Lane. Turning right, it was only a short time before they reached Swampy. Ripbag stopped and stared at the tree which had brought him into contact with Morgan on his last visit.

'What is this place?' asked Miranda. 'It feels eerie, I don't like it, let's move on.'

'How much do you know about Morgan?' asked Ripbag.

'I know lots about him, he's my brother, of course.'

'I'm not talking about the Morgan of the past. You know what happens to Polestars who do not return before the new lunar moon?' Ripbag looked straight at Miranda, his face drained of emotion and colour. 'What do you think he looks like now?'

'Stop it, Ripbag, you're frightening me. I want to go home.'

'Oh do you, well maybe you could flag down a passing battleship and ask the Frombrasent Welps to drop you off, they can be so obliging. This isn't a game, you know, and it's the wrong time to tell me you're frightened.' Ripbag turned to face the tree again.

'I've seen him Miranda, I've seen him.' The young Polestar walked around to face Ripbag, no longer showing the effects of her Istella overdose.

'What does he look like?' she stuttered.

Ripbag paused before responding. Eventually, he placed his hands on Miranda's shoulders and replied.

'He is a mutant, your brother and my best friend is a mutant, half hawk, with the mind and body of a demented Polestar. He is awesome, massive, powerful, frightening and totally unpredictable. He has become a force to be feared, he is all of these things.' Miranda sat down on the roadside, her head cradled in her hands.

'I'm sorry,' said Ripbag, 'but you need to know, for your own safety, however hard it may be to take.'

Miranda didn't respond immediately but it was clear she was shocked by Ripbag's description.

'You have a plan, right? This is going to be OK, isn't it?' asked Miranda.

'I have a plan, but no, I don't know if it will be OK. I do know that we will be in great danger. Mutant Polestars are totally unpredictable and it makes no difference whatsoever that you're his sister and you need to understand that.'

'I do, Ripbag, I've read enough about mutants back home. I just can't believe my brother is one, he must be living a nightmare.'

'Yes, but one I believe he can be awoken from,' replied Ripbag.

Miranda leaned forward making serious eye contact with Ripbag.

'I am so proud of you,' she said. 'Your loyalty to Morgan and my family is beyond all expectations and, yes, I am frightened but I will do anything to help my brother. I hope you believe that.' Ripbag didn't reply but simply put his arms around her and smiled.

'Come on, it's time we were moving on.' Secretly he knew that when it came to courage Miranda had bags of the stuff but he needed to be truthful with her, if only to prepare her for what she was about to encounter. That being achieved, both Ripbag and Miranda set off to harvest Istella in an area not too far from Conny Castle prior to their rendezvous with Jac and Wander at eight o'clock.

Chapter Seven

Hearing of Morgan's transformation to a mutant form was a difficult thing fir Miranda to deal with. However, this was nothing compared to the hardship suffered by Smirnoff on Capper.

It was truly a desperate place in every sense of the word subject to harsh cold temperatures, unpredictable climate change and desolate terrain. Capper, the star itself, was as welcoming as Red Snapper's dorsal fin.

This was typical of stars on the Capper Flow, none of which were inhabited except for Capper, which was used to imprison the criminal fraternity from Polestar communities and captive Welps. Capper was huge in terms of its size, the numbers of offenders and the prisoners of war it retained. The guardsmen on Capper totalled thousands themselves and were specially selected representatives from all the stars, although those from Alrai seemed to exceed those from other stars. Alrai guardsmen were notorious for discipline and, unlike most other guardsmen, looked forward to their stay of duty on the Capper Flow.

The work regime relentlessly enforced by the guards was unforgiving. Prisoners were chained together in pairs and retribution for acts of indiscipline by one detainee was carried out on both.

A large part of the working day was dedicated to the excavation of raw materials for use on other stars starting early in the morning and finishing late at night. This practice continued irrespective of any climatic change and it was not unusual for prisoners to perish through exhaustion, lack of Istella or dire temperatures, which were normally well below freezing. However, the guardsmen were unmoved and, without dignity, dragged those who had fallen to transportation units which disposed of their bodies. In addition, it was not unusual for prisoners to attack one another. This mainly occurred when rations of Istella were thrown to them by the guardsmen on a daily basis. Such was the need to secure Istella that fighting regularly broke out, sometimes with fatal consequences.

In the midst of this stood the forlorn figure of Smirnoff who, above all else, was secured by chains to a female Frombrasent Welp called Zalgud, who was unbelievably ugly. Along with other Polestars, Smirnoff and Zalgud were detained in one of the many large dome shaped shelters, which were two-thirds buried underground to provide some protection from the harsh elements. The top section of the dome was transparent and protruded out of the ground to provide natural light into the massive chamber.

Natural light on Capper, however, was in itself a scarce resource, as there was little difference between day and night, just a constant twilight, which gave a strange feeling of absence and disorientation. There was no segmentation or privacy for prisoners in the dome, just a large open space, which had a huge upper gallery around its perimeter and was patrolled day and night by guardsmen. The place was nothing more than a pit filled with what was considered to be the filth of the universe.

Despite her looks, which were not enhanced by an unusual branding on her neck, Zalgud did not display the normal behavioural characteristics of your average Welp. She was smart and had quickly realised, as had Smirnoff, that their chances of survival on Capper would be greater if they worked together as a team, rather than against each other as enemies. When it came to meal times for example, both Smirnoff and Zalgud would collect as much Istella and water as possible during the feeding frenzy and then retreat to a quiet section of the dome to share their spoils. This strategy worked well, as Istella provides

Polestars with all their mineral and liquid requirements without the need for water, which is the only substance consumed by the Frombrasent Welps.

Although they would never be the best of friends, this unlikely pact was paying dividends and, on the whole, from a detainee's perspective, Smirnoff and Zalgud were getting by.

On one particular evening, after retreating to a relatively quiet section of the dome to devour their spoils of Istella and water, Smirnoff engaged in inquisitive conversation with Zalgud.

'Where are you from Zalgud?' asked Smirnoff.

Zalgud raised her eyes and stared at Smirnoff, then continued to take in the water they had collected from the feeding frenzy. Although the Frombrasent Welps had been in conflict with the Polestars for many years, no one knew where they came from and Smirnoff's question was not placed interrogatively, more inquisitively.

'You must have family,' probed Smirnoff.

Zalgud stopped drinking momentarily as if fazed by the comment but then continued without response.

'My name is Smirnoff,' he continued, but before he could say more, Zalgud interrupted in a rather superior tone.

'Oh, I know who you are, Smirnoff. You're a walking miracle, slaughtered by the mighty Bolo and saved by the wondrous Auwnwanx.'

Smirnoff was gob-smacked.

'You were there, you were one of the foot soldiers at the Cassiopeia?'

'Yes, Smirnoff, I was there along with five thousand foot soldiers waiting to descend upon Sproatsville.'

'But why?' enquired Smirnoff. 'For what gain? We would never have made a deal with a rat like Bolo.'

'Ha,' huffed Zalgud. 'Don't you think we knew that? We didn't want to negotiate a deal with an inferior race, that was just a front. We wanted the Auwnwanx you idiot.' Zalgud's eyes narrowed. 'It is said that, *He who dances with fire will truly receive his greatest desire.'* This is the prophecy of the Auwnwanx. Dance in the flames of the Auwnwanx and your desire is granted. We would preside over life and death and become the supreme arbitrator. With such power we would be invincible, this is the desire of the Frombrasent Welps.'

'How do you know this?' snapped Smirnoff. 'The powers of the Auwnwanx are sacred to the Polestars. I've never heard of such a prophecy.'

'Really?' quipped Zalgud, sarcastically. 'Perhaps you should ask your friend, Ballbeagle.'

Zalgud gave a wry smile and then turned over to rest, leaving Smirnoff contemplating the meaning behind her insinuation. It would prove to be a long and restless night for him.

Having returned to Crooked Cottage from the Istella fields, Ripbag and Miranda welcomed both Jac and Wander who arrived shortly after eight o'clock, and for the first time ever, Ripbag greeted Wander by giving her a gentle kiss on the cheek. Wander couldn't believe it and her glow lit up the entrance to Ripbag's home, under the front doorstep of this beautiful dwelling.

'Thanks for coming,' he said. 'I guess you're wondering why we are here.'

'Well,' said Jac, sarcastically. 'It did rather cross our minds.'

'OK then, I'll waste no more time. I need your help, or rather we need your help, that is Miranda and I, to pull off a plan to trap Morgan.'

'Trap Morgan?' Jac said, springing to his feet.

'Yes, trap Morgan and, once trapped, I intend to use the Auwnwanx and its magical power to free Morgan and put an end to his living nightmare.'

'You're mad,' said Jac. 'Have you been ingesting too much Istella? What are you going to do? Offer him a sack of bird seed?'

'Jac,' scolded Wander. 'Show some respect.'

Jac realised his comment was hurtful to Miranda and sat down again.

'Are you serious?' asked Wander.

'I've thought of nothing else since my last visit,' said Ripbag. 'I've already enlisted the help of a few other Polestars here on assignment but I need you both to help me pull this off.'

'How exactly?' asked Wander.

Ripbag began to explain.

'The last time I was here, I saw Morgan, he was at Swampy.'

'Yes, it's rumoured he spends a lot of time in that area,' said Jac. 'So much so, that hardly anyone mines there anymore.'

'It was a chilling experience,' said Ripbag, 'and I will never forget it, but at the end of our encounter Morgan threatened me. He told me never to return to Sproatsville again and although he never said it, he implied that if I did, he would kill me. I promised I would never give up on him and I won't, that's why I am here.'

'But what is your plan Ripbag? Exactly how do you intend we should all die?' said Jac.

'The plan is relatively simple. I will use myself as the bait to attract Morgan to the Grand Old Tree. I will appear to be tied to the tree and, directly above me, will be you, Jac and Wander. You will be holding the pulley rope attached to my back harness, and at the precise moment, you will jump from the tree, hoisting me clear of Morgan's advance. A number of Polestars will show at this point whilst Morgan is against the tree and will secure him with grapple whips, pinning him to the huge trunk. Once secured, the Auwnwanx will be placed over him and my good friend will be released from his torture.'

'Crikey, Ripbag, you make it sound so simple. What if we get our timing wrong? What if we cannot secure him? He is huge!'

'I am aware of the dangers, Jac, but what if we succeed, how good would that be?'

Miranda stood up from her seat and walked over to Jacadaro.

'Please say you'll help my brother Jac, I feel sure if the tables were turned he would do the same for you.' For a moment, Jac seemed mesmerised by Miranda's plea.

'Of course I will, of course I will,' he replied.

Ripbag wasn't sure whether Jac had volunteered his services out of loyalty or desire for the young Polestar, however what mattered was that he had agreed.

'And you, Wander, are you in?'

'Just try stopping me,' she replied. Miranda screamed out in excitement and was soon joined by all the others purring in celebration of their new found collective spirit.

When the initial excitement died down, Jac asked inquisitively, 'When?'

'When what?' replied Ripbag.

'When do we do this?'

'Tomorrow evening close to midnight.'

Once again the four Polestars returned to a state of euphoria. It seemed for a short while that everyone had forgotten about the danger attached to such a daring plan and a mood of optimism prevailed. The wonderful glow from their tiny bodies was a sight to see although one could say with some certainty that by tomorrow evening their illuminated smiles would diminish through fear and trepidation as events unfolded before them.

The following day Ripbag, Jacadaro, Wander and Miranda Moon began work immediately erecting the pulley device, which would lift Ripbag to safety high into the Grand Old Tree. As soon as it was ready, a number of test runs took place to ensure Jac and Wander's combined weight was enough to launch Ripbag skyward at the appropriate moment. It was perfect, every time Jac and Wander jumped out of the tree with tackle attached, Ripbag shot up, perching himself on a major branch. As soon as that happened, Polestars appeared from all directions launching wave after wave of grapple whips which wrapped themselves around the body of the tree with great force and accuracy. It was perfect. Climbing down from the tree, Ripbag summoned everyone together.

'I just want to thank you, every single one of you for agreeing to help Morgan,' he said. 'There is no doubt you are all placing yourselves in great danger but I just know we can pull this off. In doing so we will achieve two things, firstly, the return of a loyal and faithful friend to our community and secondly, the removal of a mutant from Sproatsville, making this a safer place for all of us to visit. Is there anyone who doesn't wish to take part, or isn't clear of what is expected of them?'

Not a single Polestar responded until a little voice broke through the silence.

'Excuse me, but I'm not sure what you want me to do?'

Everyone looked down to see where this tiny voice came from. It was Miranda Moon. At first no one responded to the youngster for fear of upsetting her, as everyone shared an admiration for the courage she displayed and it was left to Ripbag to reply.

'Err, I'm sorry Miranda but we have all the volunteers we need to pull this off. It doesn't make sense to introduce danger for the sake of it.'

'Nice try, Ripbag,' she replied. 'What you really mean is you want to tuck me out of harm's way, just in case things turn nasty. After all, you wouldn't want to be held responsible for anything that happens to me would you?'

'OK,' snarled Ripbag. 'You're right. How do you think that would reflect on me with your family? Morgan is already a mutant and Ripbag had his tiny sister fed to him. No! It's not going to happen Miranda, I didn't invite you here, but now that you are, I expect you to do as you are told.'

Miranda's face turned as stony as a pebble dashed wall and her glow had all but faded to a dim flicker. In frustration and anger, she turned on her heels and stormed off in the direction of Gate Keepers Lodge.

'Don't you do anything silly, do you hear?' shouted Ripbag, but Miranda wasn't having any of it and maintained her course until she disappeared from sight.

Ripbag gathered himself and returned to the group.

'A quarter before midnight then, we all need to be in place by that time.' All the Polestars nodded their heads and then began to hug one another. They all realised that their encounter with Morgan in the coming hours would be a moment that would remain with them for the rest of their lives, assuming of course they survived past midnight. Soon, everyone departed to go about their business, except for Wander and Ripbag.

'You're going to have to be careful, Ripbag,' said Wander. 'Miranda looked very upset.'

'I can't afford for anything to happen to her, Wander, it's just not a risk I'm prepared to take,' replied Ripbag.

'Soon she will be coming here on assignment herself,' said Wander. 'Making her own way and own decisions, it's a difficult time for her, you need to understand that.'

'I do, it's just that I can do without it right now.'

Wander smiled and took hold of Ripbag's arm.

'Come on, you can walk me back to Isnthalovely.'

As they made their way towards Wander's home, the two Polestars looked as though they had been an item for years and, picking his moment, Ripbag suddenly asked Wander, 'Have you ever visited Polaris before?'

'No, never, although I've heard it's a beautiful star.'

'Oh, it is Wander, you would love it, and there is so much I'd like to show you, would you like to g.......

'Yes,' she interrupted before Ripbag could finish. Wander stopped walking and turned to face Ripbag

'I've been waiting to go for a long time, it would make me so happy.'

'Then you shall go Wander, with me when all this business with Morgan is done. I shall take you to Polaris, nothing would make me happier' purr purr...........

Soon they arrived at Isnthalovely and, after bidding farewell to Wander, Ripbag began to make his way back through the snicket which led to Swithun's Tower. Ripbag stopped and looked up towards the window near the clock which used to be the home of Bullwrinkle. Memories of this dear old Polestar came flooding back to him and Ripbag's glow began to fade.

'If only you were here now, Bullwrinkle,' he said. 'Things would seem so much clearer. What would you think of my plan, eh? Would you agree with what I am doing? Would you support me, Bullwrinkle? If only you could give me a sign.'

No sooner had Ripbag uttered these words did the Swithun's bell suddenly chime. The shock nearly bowled him over as it couldn't have come at a more timely moment. Smiling to himself, Ripbag slowly continued on his journey. As he got to the lychgate on Swithun's perimeter, he looked up at the tower again to bid farewell to his friend. It was then that he realised the large clock handle was not pointing upwards, but was a quarter of the way round. The clock only chimed on the hour and it never failed to do so.

'It's a sign,' thought Ripbag. 'Bullwrinkle is here, he's here!'

Filled with excitement, Ripbag continued his journey back to Crooked Cottage. There he would stay for the rest of the day, planning, plotting and rehearsing in his own mind how events would unfold at midnight.

Chapter Eight

All too soon, the clock in Crooked Cottage approached a quarter to midnight and Ripbag peered outside to see a group of Polestars gathered under the Grand Old Tree. Jac was up the tree pulling and tugging on the harness ropes, which had been assembled a few hours earlier.

For a moment, Ripbag wondered whether his plan to rescue Morgan really was as ludicrous as Jac had previously suggested. In spite of this, Ripbag took a deep breath, looked towards the stars and whispered to himself, 'Walk with me, Bullwrinkle, show me the way.'

Venturing outside to join his friends and colleagues, Ripbag stopped just short of the Grand Old Tree.

He raised his hands in the air and in a loud commanding voice said, 'Polestars of the Universe, greetings it is indeed a great honour to be here.'

Everyone just stood and stared at him, wondering if he had become possessed by Bullwrinkle's spirit. He was transfixed. It was like he had become Bullwrinkle himself. Eventually he lowered his hands to his side as if returning from a hypnotic state and began to embrace his friends in a show of unity.

'Is everything in place?' he asked.

'It's all in place,' replied one of the Polestars.

'And that includes the harness as well,' said Jac, lowering himself down from the tree.

'Good,' said Ripbag. 'And Wander, where is Wander?'

'I'm here, Ripbag, right beside you.'

Wander had just arrived and reassuringly put her arm around Ripbag's shoulders.

'Are you sure you want to do this?' she said quietly. 'It's not too late to reconsider.'

'I don't want to do this, Wander, but I know I have to. I couldn't live with myself knowing I had abandoned my friend.'

Wander smiled at Ripbag.

'Is everyone in place with their grapple whips?' enquired Ripbag.

At that moment, Polestars appeared from all directions with grapple whips hanging by their sides.

'We're here, Ripbag,' they shouted and quickly returned to their positions.

'Right then, it's time,' said Ripbag. 'Morgan patrols the sky soon after midnight and I need to lure him in.'

Ripbag walked towards the huge trunk of the Grand Old Tree and then turned to face his friends and colleagues. He raised his arms above his head to enable the pulley ropes to be attached to his harness and then concealed the attachments with his clothing. It was perfect. As soon as this was done, everyone ran to take up their positions. It was as if securing the harness was the point of no return and no one needed instruction telling them what to do or where to go. Wander, however, remained for a few moments.

'Go on, Wander,' said Ripbag. 'Take up your position with Jac.'

Although she tried not to show it, Wander was desperately worried about what was going to take place and felt very uncomfortable that Ripbag was being used as live bait.

'OK,' she said reluctantly, as she turned to climb the Grand Old Tree. Ripbag's eyes followed her as she made her way towards the branch where Jacadaro sat.

'Wander,' Ripbag called.

'Yes,' she replied.

'Where is Miranda?'

'I don't know, she hasn't been seen since she stormed off. She'll turn up Ripbag, please don't worry. You must focus all your attention on Morgan, do you hear?'

'I hear you, Wander, I hear you.'

Ripbag cast his eyes towards the sky, which was littered with beautiful glittering stars. It was a bizarre scene, his body positioned in the shape of a crucifix to give the impression he was defenceless and, although the place was crawling with Polestars nervously awaiting Morgan's arrival, it looked totally deserted.

They didn't have to wait too long, however, for soon after midnight the sound of the flugelhorn droned ominously. It was a sign that Morgan had been spotted and was patrolling the sky for prey. Ripbag's colour drained, as did every other Polestar's in the vicinity.

Suddenly Ripbag became aware of a movement in the moonlit sky. Something was heading his way. It must be Morgan, he thought. This is it! But, with a blink of an eye, the object seemed to disappear and Ripbag was left feeling that his fear and imagination had got the better of him. The next few minutes were unbearable and seemed to go on for eternity, as he scanned the sky for any sign of Morgan, but he was nowhere to be seen.

For one awful moment, Ripbag wondered if Morgan had landed behind him but felt sure Jac and Wander would be aware if he had.

Where could he be, will he show, thought Ripbag. 'Come on Morgan show yourself,' he whispered.

No sooner had he uttered these words, a terrifying and piercing screech echoed over Sproatsville village. It was Morgan and, for the first time since his meeting at Swampy, Ripbag had a clear view of him. Morgan too had seen Ripbag and, like a vulture circling its prey, he flew menacingly above the Grand Old Tree. He looked massive, even though he was some distance away and Ripbag wondered whether the grapple whips would hold such a creature. Clearly he had grown.

'Be still,' whispered Jac to Ripbag. 'Be still.'

There was no need to worry, however, Ripbag was about as frozen to the spot as he could be. Morgan continued to circle above and then descended, with speed and accuracy, landing on the perimeter edge of the Grand Old Tree. He thrust his head backwards, opened his wings and again screeched loudly, filling those around him with dread and horror. Morgan lurched his huge head forward to focus his eyes on Ripbag. It was like witnessing a sacrifice, with Morgan being the recipient of the spoils.

His beak was oozing saliva as he began to move towards Ripbag, his claws tearing up the ground below him with ease. Morgan had developed both physically and mentally into a more severe mutant form and he was about to tear Ripbag to pieces. He no longer knew who Ripbag was, nor did he care. Ripbag's body felt like it was about to explode with the tension.

'Hold it,' he whispered. 'Hold it, wait for my word, wait for my word.' But, just as he was about to give the command, a little voice interrupted.

'Hello, Morgan.'

Out from behind the tree stepped Miranda Moon.

'Miranda!' screamed Ripbag, 'What are you doing?'

Unmoved, Miranda continued. 'It's me Morgan your little sister, do you remember me? Sure you do, I've come to help you and to take you back home.'

'Turn back you fool, turn back,' cried Ripbag.

'It's OK, Ripbag' said Miranda. 'This is my brother and he loves me too.'

Morgan's eyes were blood red and he had turned his focus upon the little Polestar. Unfortunately for Miranda, the only love Morgan had now was ripping chunks of meat from his victims, an act he was about to perform on her. His hunting instinct could not be curtailed any longer and, with two flaps of his huge wings, launched himself at Miranda, claws wide apart.

The youngster screamed as the mutant lunged towards her but, moments before his claws punctured her tiny body, she was sent tumbling to the ground by Wander, who had dived out of the tree to help her. Morgan seized Wander firmly in his talons in exchange for Miranda. Dangling hopelessly from beneath this huge creature, Wander was beyond help.

Ripbag screamed out Wander's name, 'Oh no, please no!'

Seemingly distracted by Ripbag's plea, Morgan released Wander from his grip sending her tumbling to the ground. Morgan had seen bigger prey and he was going to have Ripbag. Realising that Ripbag was helpless and at Morgan's mercy, Miranda leapt to her feet somersaulting and spinning high into the tree, landing next to Jacadaro. Both simultaneously grabbed the pulley rope and jumped out of the tree, sending Ripbag skyward milliseconds before Morgan's claws struck deep into the bark of the Grand Old Tree.

Immediately the sound of grapple whips could be heard fizzing through the air as scores of brave Polestars launched with accuracy and power attack after attack on the mutant beast. It was a terrifying moment as grapple whips wrapped themselves around Morgan securing him firmly to the huge trunk, neutralizing the power of his wings in the process.

Morgan had been captured. In his haste to reach Wander, Ripbag had momentarily forgotten his main objective, which was to release Morgan by the power bestowed in the Auwnwanx. Time couldn't be wasted and a group of Polestars quickly took the Auwnwanx, placed it over Morgan's tethered body and stood back in anticipation.

Meanwhile, Wander lay motionless on the ground and when Ripbag reached her he could see that she had only moments to live. He was now aware that the Auwnwanx had used the last of its miraculous powers on Morgan having accessed its sorcery on three separate occasions. There was nothing he could do, absolutely nothing. He placed his hand gently under her neck and cradled her head.

'I've always loved you Wander, always, but I'm sorry I was never brave enough to say so.'

'Shush,' Wander replied. 'I always loved you too. Will you keep your promise Ripbag?'

'Anything, Wander, just say it and I'll do anything for you.'

'Take me to Polaris, just as you said you would, and lay me to rest there.'

'Of course I will, I'll be by your side forever.'

Wander raised a pitiful smile. Fumbling in his ouzybag, Ripbag reached inside and pulled out a beautifully decorated envelope. He opened it and gave the small note inside to Wander. It read, 'Together we will never be alone.' It was the handwritten note she had passed to him via Ballbeagle at the end of his last visit.

'You keep it, Ripbag, keep it forever.'

Wander held out her hand affectionately touching Ripbag's fingertips but there was no warmth or glow. Her eyes closed and she passed away.

Unnoticed by Ripbag, all the other Polestars had gathered in a circle around them both and stood in silence out of respect for Wander, all except Miranda Moon who was sobbing uncontrollably.

After a short while, the silence was broken by one of the Polestars who moved forward and placed his hand on Ripbag's shoulder. Ripbag slowly rose to his feet and turned his head to face the Polestar offering support. It was none other than his great friend, Morgan.

The awesome power of the Auwnwanx had released him from his torment having met all three conditions. What was to be a moment of elation, however, was somehow lost. The pain of Wander's death had nullified the euphoria of freeing Morgan and Ripbag felt emotionally drained. Morgan embraced Ripbag in a show of gratitude and respect and, with tears of sadness and joy, Ripbag responded. No words were exchanged and at that moment in time, none would have had meaning or value. The objective of Ripbag's assignment had been realised.

In time, the scale of achievement in Ripbag's visit to Sproatsville would become legendary and would clearly go down in Polestar history. All those involved in the daring rescue of Morgan were heroes and that included Miranda Moon. Whilst her interference may have caused the death of Wander, her bravery was acknowledged by most as exceptional, especially in the face of such danger and for such a youngster too.

Ripbag, unintentionally on his part, had established himself as the Polestar most likely to fill the void left by Bullwrinkle in Sproatsville but only time would tell. His determination to lead the rescue mission for Morgan, along with his success as Polestar Prince, brought him much respect and admiration from within the Polestar community and would have met with approval from Bullwrinkle himself.

In the days leading up to their departure from Sproatsville, Ripbag, Morgan and Miranda Moon spent countless hours revisiting the events of the past lunar months and especially those of the last few days. Their recollections and stories were filled with happiness and remorse and, if anything, helped to reinforce the bond between them, which in the Polestar community was so necessary for friendships to be sustained.

It had come to light however, that Miranda's interference in the rescue mission was nothing to do with irresponsibility or youthful exuberance, but more to do with influence and persuasion. Miranda had explained to Ripbag that when she stormed off to Gatekeepers Lodge, she met another Polestar previously unknown to her, who seemed to know her name. Miranda and the stranger had spent a long time talking and he persuaded her that Morgan would react sympathetically towards his sister and that she should seize the opportunity to talk to him. That was the reason why she intervened on that fateful evening.

Ripbag was left confused and worried, for the description Miranda had provided of the stranger was none other than Ballbeagle. How could this be? thought Ripbag. Ballbeagle was not on assignment, he was not in the assignment book and, in any event, he was a friend, surely he wouldn't do such a thing? Nevertheless, Ripbag knew he couldn't leave the matter to rest and at the first opportunity he would confront Ballbeagle to settle his mind.

Soon enough, the time had come for Ripbag and his friends to leave Sproatsville and to enter the gravity corridor. All arrangements were in place and Ripbag, Morgan and Miranda Moon were gathered at the flag pole on Sproatsville green. Alongside Ripbag was the body of his beloved Wander and, like Bullwrinkle's, her casket had been ceremoniously decorated to represent her heroic status. Wander was to be taken to Polaris, as she had requested and would remain a part of Ripbag's life forever. Although Wander had told Ripbag to keep the tiny envelope which contained their loving message to one another, he felt it should stay with Wander wherever her soul may travel and he placed it in a tiny pocket on her gown.

Once again, his departure from Sproatsville involved the transportation of a loved one under his care through the gravity corridor to a final resting place, an event which most Polestars rarely experience at all. The only reassurance on this occasion was that he was supported by his long time friend, Morgan. There was to be no great ceremony to mark this occasion as Ripbag, Morgan and Miranda locked arms in anticipation of their forthcoming journey. No sooner had Ripbag touched Wander's casket did the gravity corridor open and the journey to Polaris began.

Chapter Nine

Another gruelling day had come to pass on Capper and the Alrai guardsmen in particular had ensured the regime of punishment and hard work continued relentlessly. More often than not, Smirnoff was the focus of attention with some Alrai guardsmen, as they were particularly hard on those offenders from their own star, viewing Smirnoff as a slur on their reputation. This didn't go down too well with Zalgud, as she was also on the receiving end of any untoward treatment because she was chained to Smirnoff.

On this particular day, however, both Smirnoff and Zalgud had avoided bullying and beatings and were resting against the dome wall recuperating from their day's labour. Their strategy of working together at feeding time was still proving advantageous and, compared to other prisoners who adopted less calculated approaches, they were surviving.

One could not describe the relationship that existed between Zalgud and Smirnoff as friendly but clearly they were getting along better than before and examples of co-operation between them were becoming more frequent.

'Are you awake Zalgud?' asked Smirnoff. There was no reply. Smirnoff waited a while and then laid his head back against the wall, staring tediously at the massive dome ceiling.

'What do you want?' Zalgud replied unexpectedly.

'Ballbeagle,' replied Smirnoff. 'Talk to me about Ballbeagle.'

'Why should I?' she replied.

'Well, we've both got nothing to lose,' said Smirnoff. 'Neither of us are going anywhere.'

Zalgud's long neck rose up like a serpent and her piercing eyes threw Smirnoff a look that could kill at ten paces.

'It was perfect,' she began. 'Armed with information about Morgan's disappearance, we were able to devise a plan which would enable the almighty Welps to descend upon your Cassiopeia in relative safety and seize the magical Auwnwanx. Once in our possession, a massive fleet of battleships, strong enough to overpower any resistance on Sproatsville, were at our disposal ready for battle.

'But why?' asked Smirnoff. 'The Polestar fraternity would have retaliated and your victory would have been short-lived.'

'Really?' said Zalgud. 'With knowledge of the Auwnwanx prophecy and our desire to rule over life and death, we would have been immortal. Your beloved Sproatsville, with its rich resources of Istella, would have been in the control of one Council headed up by one person, an ally of the Welps.

'Ballbeagle!' gasped Smirnoff.

'How quick you are, Smirnoff, your reputation is confirmed. Yes, Ballbeagle, he'd rather hoped that you would assist him in his plans, just as he has been assisting us for some time. His vision of ruling Sproatsville on behalf of Aldermin would have been realised if it wasn't for that hideous creature taking our immaculate leader from us,' snarled Zalgud.

There was a short silence as Zalgud, who had become quite irate, gathered herself.

'A temporary blip, that's all, a temporary blip, Smirnoff. Ballbeagle is still an ally and soon enough the Polestar empire will be a shadow of its former self.'

For a moment Zalgud had forgotten the relationship that had developed between herself and Smirnoff and was her old self, manipulative, evil and not to be trusted. Smirnoff would do well to remember that. Most, if not all Welps, craved power and control and Zalgud was no different.

Returning to her previous position, Zalgud fell to rest, leaving Smirnoff in disbelief of Ballbeagle's treachery. How could he do this? he thought, and why would he assume I would assist him?

Smirnoff cast his mind back to the Cassiopeia and to the moment when Ballbeagle intervened between Jacadaro and himself. Recalling Ballbeagle's comment *'No need for thanks, Smirnoff, just remember who your real friends are, you never know when you might need them.'*

Smirnoff slowly began to realise that Ballbeagle was suggesting the favour may need to be returned one day and why shouldn't he? I am a thief after all, thought Smirnoff, a criminal, no one would want to know me and my only friend would be Ballbeagle, another criminal, only his plan backfired.

What can I do? thought Smirnoff. I have to escape to inform Ripbag, I must escape! As he repeated this pledge, like Zalgud he drifted into a deep, if not troubled sleep.

In the weeks leading up to the arrival of fresh supplies and new prisoners on Capper, which involved the changing of guardsmen, Smirnoff had been busy plotting his escape from Capper. In fact, he had barely thought of anything else since Zalgud had enlightened him of Ballbeagle's treachery. Perhaps unsurprisingly, his escape plan required the co-operation of Zalgud, who was more than a willing partner, and who had secured Smirnoff's word that upon reaching Polaris she would be free to return to her star, wherever that may be. Smirnoff's plan was to escape to Polaris and not Alrai, his own star, by stowing away in one of the returning supply ships. There, he intended to meet up with Ripbag to inform him about Ballbeagle's plan to rule Sproatsville although he wasn't quite sure just how he was going to do this.

At long last, the supply crafts had entered Capper's flight path and by the end of the day Smirnoff and Zalgud would either be on their way to Polaris, or dead. Failure to escape would not see them ushered back to the dome to continue their sentence, instead they would be executed by the guardsmen and exhibited for all to see.

And so it began, the drone from the transporter craft carrying new Polaris guardsmen and prisoners could be heard high above the dome as it gradually descended to the ground. Shortly after, one by one, the prisoners emerged from the craft escorted by guards to a segregation unit, where the process of partnering would be completed. Once shackled, the prisoners would be allocated to a zone on Capper and finally to a dome where their sentence would begin.

Before this occurred, however, the changing of the guard would take place where the new incoming complement would replace the old and this specific procedure formed the nucleus of Smirnoff's daring escape plan. He knew the returning guardsmen for Polaris would have one thing on their mind and that was to leave Capper. Whilst they were loyal in their duty, they were not as dedicated as the Alrai guardsmen, especially at this stage of their assignment and the opportunity for escape was potentially at its greatest. Prior to the changing of the guard, the departing guardsmen had one last duty to complete before commencing their journey homeward. This was the feeding of prisoners. As usual, it was a frenzy completed in half the time it would normally take and without any real attention being paid to head count or what was going on below in the main chamber of the dome. Smirnoff and Zalgud were going to seize their opportunity.

Their first objective was to escape the dome via the labyrinth of tunnels which led either to external mining zones on Capper or to operational facilities and services used by the guardsmen. Escaping onto Capper was not part of their plan, as the cold harsh climate would almost certainly kill them. They needed, therefore, to reach the tunnel which led them to the boarding gates of the returning supply ship to Polaris.

Smirnoff was familiar with the route, as he'd seen so many prisoners come and go over the months and he was also familiar with the ergonomics of the craft, which provided ample opportunity for stowaway. As an Alrai Polestar, he had served with the transporter service and if necessary could actually pilot the ship. The difficult part, however, was getting out of the dome undetected and then releasing themselves from the shackles restraining them.

Instead of fighting for Istella and water with the other prisoners, Smirnoff and Zalgud picked up small amounts and sat down against the dome wall next to a pair of interlocking sliding doors. It was normal practice that after each feeding frenzy, the guards would enter through the doors to check on the prisoners. The official reason was to undertake a roll call, but in reality it was to remove any fatalities which may have occurred in the struggle to secure food. The procedure was always the same, a guard would enter through the first set of doors and only when they had closed behind him would the second set open, giving access to the dome. Other guardsmen would patrol the upper tier armed with H.I.T. guns. Prisoners would scurry to the outer wall of the dome, falling in line for the roll call and any disobedience would be dealt with severely.

Smirnoff and Zalgud simply stood up and took their place close to the doors. The guardsman hurriedly began to walk the circumference of the wall, counting out aloud for each prisoner present, whilst his colleagues patrolled high above. It was obvious he was in a rush to complete this task and whilst doing so, Zalgud carefully placed a piece of her sharp claws into the corner of the track upon which the second set of interlocking doors ran. This was easily achieved, as the doors remained open whilst the guard entered the dome to enable a quick retreat. The claw was attached to a length of plaited mane hair, which was almost invisible to the eye.

Once the roll call was finished, the guard immediately turned on his heel and stood between the two sets of double doors, one set behind him open, the other in front closed. His impatience was building as he waited for the doors behind him to close, which would automatically trigger the release of the retaining front set. Eventually, the rear doors closed, but upon impact with Zalgud's claw, immediately opened again in unison with the front set. The guardsman was totally oblivious to what had just happened as he exited the enclosure briskly, screaming with delight at the prospect of his service on Capper coming to an end.

Seizing their chance, both Zalgud and Smirnoff dashed quickly into the corridor, tugging the hair rigged claw behind them. In a flash, both sets of doors crashed closed sealing in the rest of the prisoners and without a guardsman in sight.

Smirnoff and Zalgud stood rigid against the opposite facing wall of the dome in shock at what they had just done. This was not a good time, however, to reflect upon their achievement as they were in greater danger now than ever before of being spotted. They must navigate the tunnels quickly and locate the transporter craft, which would return them to Polaris. Hindered by their chains, they moved clumsily, keeping close to the wall and finding cover in the dimly lit crevasses of the tunnels. They eventually came across signs showing directions to the Alrai transporter terminal.

For a moment Smirnoff felt torn between wanting to return to his own star and fulfilling his plan to travel to Polaris. But Zalgud pulled irritably at the chains which secured them together intimating that, of all the Polestar terminals, they really didn't want to be hanging around the one used by Alrai guardsmen. They wasted no more time and soon arrived at the tunnel which would lead them to the transporter section for Polaris.

Voices seemed to be reverberating all around them, as the network of tunnels amplified the laughter and conversation generated by guardsmen close by. Unable to determine whether these sounds came from their escape tunnel only served to increase their sense of fear and disorientation. Boldly, they continued on their way until they reached a stairway which took them down to the cargo section of the Polaris transporter craft. Smirnoff's plan was to stow away in the cargo hold of the transporter. He knew that this area would not be accessed during the return journey to Polaris and so was a relatively safe haven for them. Right now, however, he still couldn't believe that his plan was still on track.

Smirnoff and Zalgud felt a sense of achievement running through their bodies and, encouraged by this, became even more determined to see their plan through.

After carefully negotiating the steps before them, they found themselves in the heart of logistical operations. In front of them stood a huge Polaris supply ship in all its glory being loaded with returns by just two guardsmen. At this point, neither Smirnoff nor Zalgud had the faintest idea how they were going to bypass the guardsmen undetected and their escape plan was now based solely on opportunity and luck. They hadn't expected to get this far, but they had, and they were metres away from pulling it off.

Suddenly the two guardsmen reappeared pulling a large container which they left at the side of the cargo hold. Zalgud gingerly pushed her long neck out from the cover of the stairwell to get a better view and furtively informed Smirnoff what she could see.

'Um, the containers are used to transport provisions to and from our stars,' whispered Smirnoff. 'And they are very large.'

As he spoke, two more containers arrived which were hooked up to form a chain. The latter two containers, they noted, were sealed with tape marked 'Security Checked.' The first two were not.

'Of course!' exclaimed Smirnoff. 'The containers, we could hide in the containers. Once inside the hold no one will bother inspecting them and they will be stored at the main compound on Polaris.'

Smirnoff and Zalgud waited until the guardsmen left to fetch more containers, then hastily made their way to where the containers stood. Using a razor sharp claw, Zalgud scored a line through the centre of the security tape which sealed the lid to the main body. Smirnoff stood close by her side nervously fidgeting, whilst keeping watch for the guardsmen. Zalgud was just tall enough to open the lid and peer inside.

'It's half full,' she said. 'Dirty laundry, it's dirty laundry!'

This was perfect, not only was there space to stow away but there was also material to cover their bodies.

Without hesitation, Zalgud launched herself to the top, diving head first into the laundry forgetting momentarily that she was attached to Smirnoff and he was unceremoniously catapulted into the container, landing spread eagled across her body.

'Thanks for the warning,' scowled Smirnoff, as he pulled himself embarrassingly from Zalgud's ugly face.

'You're in the box, aren't you?' she replied. 'Now stop moaning and close the lid quickly!'

Smirnoff sprang to his feet and lowered the lid swiftly, but quietly, into place. The edges of the tape joined perfectly showing no evidence of tamper or its cargo now safely inside. Covering themselves with dirty laundry, Smirnoff and Zalgud wriggled like worms to the bottom of the container until they were out of sight and, sure enough, it wasn't long before they could hear the footsteps of the returning guardsmen coming their way.

'Hurry up,' cried one of the guards. 'We just need to security check the first container and connect up to the pulley.'

It was obvious that they were eager to get on with things to speed up their exit from Capper. Smirnoff could hear the tape being sealed around the other containers and was fearful that they would return to check the one they were hiding in, but they didn't. In fact, without warning, there was a jolt followed by the screeching of wheels as the convoy of containers was slowly drawn into the cargo hold. Smirnoff and Zalgud stared at each other in disbelief as their escape from Capper was all but achieved.

With a dull thud, the main doors of the cargo hold shut tight and ironically their exit from Capper was now down to the very guardsmen who were responsible for their detention.

Meanwhile, life on Polaris was pretty good. It was just as Ripbag had described it to Wander - a beautiful star inhabited by billions of Polestars which gave it its characteristic yellow glow, visible to all others in the universe.

Life for Ripbag wasn't bad either after the traumatic events of the last visit to Sproatsville.

Although he would never get over Wander's death, he had started to come to terms with his loss and had begun to integrate and contribute again within his community.

As for Miranda, she was now accepted as a mature Polestar who would be nominated to represent Polaris on future assignments, bearing in mind her daring, if not infamous exploits to rescue her brother, Morgan. For this, her father had finally forgiven her, although he held a degree of regret for his daughter's contribution to Wander's death, which he was reminded of each time he saw her beautifully embalmed body in the transparent cask where she was laid to rest. This sadness was always lifted, however, when Morgan was around. Even now his family could not quite believe he was alive, bearing in mind his brush with Red Snapper and transformation to a mutant form. Yes, life was pretty good.

During the day, both Ripbag and Morgan worked at the services complex which was the master base for Polaris forces. As young fit Polestars, their primary role was to service the fleet of flight crafts returning from duty.

Work was varied, providing them with opportunities for learning and today was no different to any other day when crafts returned from their missions. Ripbag and Morgan had been placed on replenishment duties which included tasks such as stock check and the topping up of cargo provisions. The latter wasn't Ripbag's favourite duty, as he found it boring and unchallenging, which was why he would draw straws with Morgan to decide who would undertake this job. Today he had drawn the short straw and was busy unloading the cargo from ships that had returned to Polaris overnight.

The last of his tasks was to remove and empty the large containers and to replenish them with stock for the return journey to Capper. He started by lowering the front flap of the first container, which was stuffed with dirty linen and began raking out the full contents onto the floor. He then turned his attention to the second container and once again he lowered the front flap. As it fell to the ground, the vibration and shudder loosened the laundry sheets, which fell away to reveal the terrified face of Smirnoff.

'Hello Smirnoff,' said Ripbag as he caught a fleeting glimpse.

'Hello, Ripbag,' said the head, which looked like it had been severed and stuck in the middle of a linen collage.

'Yikes, Smirnoff,' screamed Ripbag. 'It's really you. Wh..Wh..What are you doing in a container?'

'Yeah, and why aren't you on Capper?' asked Morgan arriving hastily.

Smirnoff was stunned at seeing Morgan but just as he was about to reply, the laundry around his head totally collapsed revealing the ominous face and neck of Zalgud.

'Ahhhhh!' screamed Ripbag and Morgan, drawing their H.I.T. guns from their holsters, pointing them straight between Zalgud's eyes.

Smirnoff lunged forward, 'No, don't shoot' he pleaded throwing himself in front of Zalgud. 'Please don't shoot, just give me time to explain. I can explain everything to you, please!'

Ripbag and Morgan noticed the shackles that bound Smirnoff and Zalgud and in doing so slowly lowered their guns to their sides.

'Morgan, close the cargo doors,' instructed Ripbag. Then, raising his gun again, Ripbag ordered Smirnoff and Zalgud to move slowly to the centre of the cargo hold and to sit down.

'Oh, and I mean slowly, Smirnoff, do you understand?'

'I understand, Ripbag, I understand.'

Once in the centre of the hold, Ripbag and Morgan, still with guns drawn, pulled up two boxes and sat down. They couldn't believe their eyes, sitting in front of them was a fugitive from Capper shackled to a Frombrasent Welp, the most feared and formidable enemy of any Polestar. Gradually, the glow began to return to their faces, although Smirnoff looked like a grey day around Windy Gap.

'Go on then, Smirnoff, explain why you and a Frombrasent Welp just happen to be inside the guts of a Polaris supply ship? Oh, and Smirnoff, unlike your normal drab performance, try to make this entertaining.'

Smirnoff began, and for once in his life, he really couldn't stop. He told of Ballbeagle's plan to rule Sproatsville and of his allegiance with the Frombrasent Welps and how they came to know about Morgan's disappearance. He told of Ballbeagle's timely intervention at the Cassiopeia when Jacadaro was going to rip Smirnoff apart for stealing Istella and of his meetings with foot soldiers down Boggle Lane. And finally he told of the Frombrasent Welps' intention to steal the Auwnwanx.

'Steal the Auwnwanx!' exclaimed Ripbag. 'Never, they will never own the Auwnwanx!'

'They say the Auwnwanx has a prophecy known only to a few which, if discovered, will make you invincible,' said Smirnoff.

'What prophecy?' asked Morgan.

Smirnoff quoted Zalgud word for word, '*He who dances with fire will truly receive his greatest desire.*'

'Bullwrinkle!' gasped Ripbag.

'What was that?' said Morgan.

'Those were his last words to me, '*He who dances with fire will truly receive his greatest desire.*'

Ripbag turned his attention towards Zalgud.

'Is this true?' he snapped.

Zalgud focused her evil eyes upon Ripbag and after a few uncomfortable moments replied, 'I will tell you nothing, Ripbag, other than you would be wise to listen to Smirnoff.'

Her glare then softened as she hung her head down to the ground.

Ripbag began to reflect upon previous visits to Sproatsville and certain occurrences involving Ballbeagle, for example, his sudden appearance that day at Gatekeepers Lodge when Ripbag first arrived on assignment. He had frightened the life out of Ripbag. Had he been tracking him? he wondered. What was he doing there? And how he shared Smirnoff's dark secret of dishonesty so easily with Ripbag. Was this to blacken Smirnoff's name so much that he would only have Ballbeagle as a friend?

What about the meeting with Ballbeagle in Swampy when taking cover from the Welps.

Had he been with the foot soldiers? Finally there was Miranda's description of the Polestar who encouraged her to gate-crash the rescue of Morgan.

Chillingly, it all began to fall into place. Ripbag's face lost its glow again, not because he was scared, but because he was so angry and felt so let down. How could Ballbeagle do this and why didn't he see through him?

'Ballbeagle was a loyal and trusted friend,' said Morgan. 'You had no reason to think ill of him.'

Ripbag looked at Morgan with a very stony face.

'If it wasn't for Ballbeagle, Wander would still be alive today, she would be here.'

'Yes,' said Morgan regrettably. 'So what do we do now?'

'We must inform the Polaris Council, they will have to be told,' replied Ripbag.

'And these two, what do we do with them?'

'The Council will have to decide their fate.'

'No,' yelled Smirnoff. 'I gave my word.'

'Gave your word?' said Ripbag. 'To whom?'

'Without Zalgud I could not have escaped from Capper and without my escape you would be none the wiser of Ballbeagle's plans. I promised Zalgud that if she helped me escape I would guarantee her freedom. If you take her to the Council, she will be slaughtered.'

'Oh I see,' replied Morgan. 'You are asking us to just let her go. So how do you think that will reflect upon us? We will be seen as assisting the enemy, a Frombrasent Welp.'

Smirnoff became irate.

'If it wasn't for Zalgud we would know nothing about the Welps' desire to possess the Auwnwanx. She goes free, I demand it.'

'Demand,' said Morgan. 'I really don't see how an escaped fugitive from Capper is in a position to demand anything.'

'Be quiet both of you,' snapped Ripbag. 'I can't think.'

Ripbag strolled slowly towards the transporter doors and rested his head against them, deep in thought. After a few moments, he turned to face Smirnoff and Zalgud.

'There is only one person who can decide your fate and that's Manangos, head of the ruling Council on Polaris.

'I'm sorry Smirnoff, but until then, you and Zalgud will have to remain in custody,' and with that they were led off to one of the secure units within the complex.

Chapter Ten

Time, as always, seemed to fly by in Sproatsville and the Polestar calendar which had been full of meetings and social gatherings was once again heading to the greatest event of them all, the Cassiopeia.

An intoxicating atmosphere simmered as Polestars purred and talked about who they thought might become Polestar Prince or Princess and the celebration to follow.

Ballbeagle had been extremely busy during this time and had made countless visits back to Sproatsville on behalf of his star, Aldermin. During these visits, he had begun to play a leading role in events attempting to fill the void left by the wonderful charismatic Bullwrinkle. This was compounded by the many meetings co-ordinated by Ballbeagle under the Grand Old Tree and the gradual programme of change he was introducing, which was seen by many as exciting.

Ballbeagle had also taken to wearing a self-styled robe, similar to the one worn by Bullwrinkle, which set him aside from others and, when presenting from under the Grand Old Tree, gave him a sense of authority. Because of this, a group of Polestars had begun to form an allegiance with Ballbeagle, always supporting his proposals and never too far away from his side. By doing this, they too felt as if their status on Sproatsville had been greatly enhanced, although none of them in the past would have been portrayed as model Polestars of good character, indeed some had questionable loyalties. None of these Polestars for instance were present or provided any assistance to Ripbag, during Morgan's daring rescue some months earlier.

Motivated by his elevated profile and by the positive climate generated by the Cassiopeia, Ballbeagle was once again entertaining and enthusing others from his soap box under the Grand Old Tree. His body was glowing with excitement as he whipped the crowd into a frenzy in anticipation of the forthcoming Cassiopeia.

Clearly Polestars were inspired by Ballbeagle, who had changed to a statesman-like figure commanding respect and attention. When the pitch was at its highest, this calculating Polestar, who had become the shrewdest of operators, began to propose change, dramatically affecting the way business was conducted in Sproatsville and had been for thousands of years. In the euphoria, scores upon scores of Polestars roared their approval by chanting his name, a feat which hadn't occurred in Sproatsville since the golden days of Bullwrinkle.

In full flow, Ballbeagle proposed that preferential mining rights would be awarded to the new Polestar Prince or Princess and to the second and third place runners-up.

'It's time we all began to share in the success of the Cassiopeia,' he declared.

New signing-in measures would be introduced when on assignment to control the mining fields and this would take place in a new magnificent complex to be erected underground and beneath the Grand Old Tree.

'For how long do we have to live under structures created by humans for humans? We deserve better, much better, it's time Sproatsville had its own infrastructure to support and administer the thousands of Polestars who inhabit and visit the Istella fields, led by someone with vision and a desire to succeed. Is this the new Sproatsville we all want?'

'Yes,' screamed the crowd, loving every minute of Ballbeagle's delivery.

'Keep it coming, Ballbeagle, we're with you all the way,' yelled one onlooker.

'Who will help me build this future?' cried Ballbeagle.

Once again scores of Polestars subscribed to Ballbeagle's rhetoric.

'We will, we will,' they declared

'And who do you want as your head elect?'

'You, Ballbeagle, we want you!'

Ballbeagle's name echoed around Sproatsville and seemed to reverberate into the depths of the universe. It was almost as if he had just been pronounced Polestar Prince. Feeling elated and triumphant, Ballbeagle purred approvingly, gazed towards the stars and whispered under his breath 'then you shall have me, Sproatsville, you shall have me.' With that he turned and disappeared into the group of Polestars with whom he had forged allegiance and who by now were beginning to act like a self-imposed ruling Council. For the rest of the day, Ballbeagle would plan and plot events which would lead up to the Cassiopeia, including those propositions which would bring inevitable change to Sproatsville. A change Ballbeagle so clearly desired.

'Silence,' cried the voice from the centre of the large horseshoe table. Immediately both Smirnoff and Zalgud stopped talking and stood upright. It was Manangos, the head of the ruling Council on Polaris, a powerful and respected leader amongst the Polestar fraternity.   Having heard of the claims of treachery and treason levelled against Ballbeagle, Manangos was keen to meet Smirnoff and Zalgud and for them to appear in front of the other ruling Council Heads.

It was an awesome and intimidating sight, with many notable personalities present. The wild and brilliant Caramilla from Vega, the enigmatic Rosco from Kochab and the Great Goggo from Alrai, to name but a few, were all gathered and present waiting to hear first hand Smirnoff's story.   There was, however, no representative from Aldermin. The meeting had been arranged in great secrecy and Kro was not invited.

Poor Smirnoff looked like a wet rag hung out to dry and his glow was more akin to a flickering candle on its last drop of wax. As for Zalgud, she too was clearly dispirited but managed to show a degree of arrogance by standing tall and looking straight at Manangos. In spite of this front, she was wondering whether escaping Capper into the clutches of Manangos was really such a good idea after all and perhaps she would have been better staying put.   However, she was here and so was Smirnoff, who had begun his stuttering rendition of events.

He told of Ballbeagle's treachery and his plans to rule Sproatsville with the help of the Frombrasent Welps and, having discovered this, of his own plan to escape to Polaris with the help of Zalgud. If he was lucky enough to reach Polaris he then intended to seek out Ripbag to warn him of the ghastly goings-on in Sproatsville.

'Your actions are to be commended,' said the Great Goggo. 'But why should we believe a thief, especially one who disgraced the name of Alrai?'

Smirnoff's head dropped. Manangos then turned to Zalgud.

'Is all this true?' he scowled. Zalgud was visibly shaken by his tone.

'I have assisted Smirnoff's escape and you have heard his account of events, I owe you nothing more,' she said.

'I presume you value your life?' replied Manangos with a menacing air.

'I gave Zalgud my word that no harm would come to her,' pleaded Smirnoff. 'She has done all that was asked of her, she owes us no more.'

'Perhaps you should explain that to the Polestars of Thurban,' said Caramilla.

Thurban was, of course, Bullwrinkle's star and Zalgud was one of the foot soldiers present on that fateful day in Sproatsville.

Manangos stared at Zalgud intensely.

'We have every reason to hand you over to the guardsmen of Thurban and perhaps we should. Smirnoff's pleas, however, have more merit attached to them than even he is aware. Only a small number of Welps are branded with the sign of the preceptress, which indicates status of the highest order in your kingdom. You are more than just a foot soldier, Zalgud, you are the equivalent of royalty on Earth, a Polestar Princess amongst Polestars and without doubt a prize catch.'

Smirnoff couldn't believe his ears, all this time he'd been hobnobbing with royalty. He often wondered what the branding was on her neck but Zalgud had always avoided discussing it, and now, even in the face of clear accusation, she remained tight-lipped.

'Err, may I speak?' requested Ripbag humbly.

'Go ahead, Ripbag,' Manangos replied.

'This is the second time I have heard Smirnoff's story and, like you, at first it all seemed somewhat far-fetched to me too. However, I believe it's true.'

Gasps of disbelief echoed around the great hall, which was packed to the rafters with onlookers.

'Ballbeagle was my friend but there are too many coincidences, too many facts for this to be ignored. Smirnoff may be a thief and Zalgud an enemy but their story has many links to previous occurrences in Sproatsville, especially the rescue of Morgan. Miranda's description of the Polestar who encouraged her to gate-crash events was undoubtedly that of Ballbeagle and if so he is not only a traitor, he is personally responsible for the death of Wander. He must be stopped and brought to justice.'

During the silence which followed, Manangos slowly turned his head towards the other Council leaders, their expressions needed no vote of opinion. He then turned to face Ripbag and in a quiet, yet imposing voice said, 'Then he will be. Ripbag prepare yourself for a trip to Sproatsville.'

The Heads of Council stood up from their seats and followed Manangos into his chambers, where they would plot and outline their response to Ballbeagle's contrived and deceitful plans. Sadly for Smirnoff and Zalgud, they were led off into less exuberant surroundings under lock and key, none the wiser of their destiny. However, for the moment, Smirnoff appeared to have saved Zalgud's life, certainly in the short term, although without guarantee for longer term survival.

It was agreed by the Heads of Council that, due to Ripbag's previous association with Ballbeagle and the fact that he knew the terrain of Sproatsville particularly well, he would travel through the gravity corridor where he would rendezvous with Jacadaro. They would then both put in place a plan to secure the safety of the Auwnwanx and the downfall of Ballbeagle. A massive fleet of Polestar forces would travel to Sproatsville to engage any threat from the Frombrasent Welps. Ripbag would also take Morgan, Smirnoff, Zalgud and Miranda. Smirnoff for his knowledge of Bluebell Wood, Zalgud as a bargaining tool should it be necessary, Miranda to identify Ballbeagle as the Polestar who encouraged her to sabotage Morgan's rescue and Morgan as back-up for any eventualities that might occur.

For his part, and his efforts to forewarn the Polestar communities of Ballbeagle's treachery, Smirnoff would receive a pardon from his sentence on Capper from the Great Goggo, subject to a successful outcome to this assignment. For the moment, however, he was still considered a criminal.

All five were prepared for their journey through the gravity corridor which was going to be a real experience for Zalgud. Being a Frombrasent

Welp, she could not make this trip alone, as only Polestars have that special privilege. However, by holding hands with a Polestar, who had been authorised to travel to Sproatsville, it was possible. Her journey was not going to be made easy however as she was blindfolded and still shackled to Smirnoff which would not make for a comfortable landing.

Nevertheless, as it had done for thousands of years, the gravity corridor opened right on time sending them all hurtling towards Sproatsville and, regrettably, right in the middle of Swampy. They landed with an enormous splash shooting swirls of black swamp mud high into the branches of the trees. Brilliant, thought Ripbag, now I'll have to return to this smelly pit to get back!

For Morgan, the place had a darker and more sinister side to it. This was where he resided when trapped in a hideous mutant form hunting for prey high in the sky. He just wanted to get out of there as quickly as he had arrived.

There was something of a bonus in it for Zalgud, however. She had landed on soft terrain, although her appearance was certainly not that associated with her status, thought Smirnoff. Slowly she emerged looking somewhat undignified and shocked but, along with the others, began to make tracks towards Crooked Cottage.

'Come on,' said Ripbag. 'The sooner we get there the sooner we can clean ourselves down and prepare for the Cassiopeia.'

It was a relatively short journey to Crooked Cottage from Swampy, which was good news for Smirnoff, who was leading Zalgud gingerly by the shackles. Soon they arrived and quickly secured themselves inside the step to the main entrance where Ripbag lived.

Ripbag's next mission was to sign himself in the assignment book as soon as possible and then to put in place the plan to ensnare Ballbeagle. As he gazed out of a gap through the slab top of his home towards the Grand Old Tree, it occurred to him that all this felt rather familiar reliving the moment he stepped out to rescue Morgan on his last visit. But there was no time to dwell on the past and Manangos certainly wouldn't thank him for doing so.

Ripbag quickly settled everyone down, gave Morgan the responsibility for the Auwnwanx and instructed Smirnoff to guard Zalgud. To do this Smirnoff had to be released from the shackles which bound him to Zalgud and their removal brought him a new sense of freedom something he had lost since his deportation to Capper some months earlier.

Unfortunately for Zalgud, the shackles which were attached to Smirnoff were now locked onto a metal retaining ring deeply embedded in the wall of the concrete step. Clearly she was going nowhere. No duty was given to Miranda Moon although on this occasion she was careful not to make a fuss about that.

Eventually, Ripbag made his way out of Crooked Cottage towards the Grand Old Tree. It looked magnificent and seemed to dwarf everything around it. But something wasn't quite right. The landscape around the tree had changed, it looked very different.

As Ripbag drew closer he came to a small opening which had been carved under the roots of the tree. The opening had a stairway at the bottom which opened into a wider space. Ripbag continued onward and couldn't believe what he saw. In front of him stood the beginnings of a huge development stretching far and wide with majestic palatial buildings fit for a Council Head. A new city had grown underground with Polestars scurrying around working long into the night.

Somewhat disorientated Ripbag looked down towards the ground and stooped to pick up a small stand near to his feet. On closer inspection he realised this was the stand which had supported the assignment book for many years and was made by Bullwrinkle as a young Polestar. It was bent and twisted and had been discarded. Whoever could have done this? thought Ripbag as he cleaned the dirt and grime from its carvings. But it wasn't long before his feeling of disappointment turned to animosity and revulsion.

'How yer doing buddy?' a familiar voice came from behind.

Ripbag's expression immediately changed, it was Ballbeagle.

'Long time no see,' said Ballbeagle as Ripbag turned to face him. Ballbeagle's hand was outstretched awaiting Ripbag's fingertips in the customary way.

'Yes, long time no see,' replied Ripbag forcing a smile then turning back immediately. Ballbeagle could see Ripbag was searching for something and assumed this to be the reason why his greeting was rebuked.

'Err, I can't seem to find the assignment book, Ballbeagle, why is that?'

'Oh things have changed since the last time you were here' replied Ballbeagle.

'Polestars wanted change, they needed change and, as you can see, they are getting change.'

'My goodness,' replied Ripbag. 'It seems you have changed too, Ballbeagle.'

'Yes, I've been given a new lease of life, Ripbag. The Polestars of Sproatsville needed someone to lead them, to drive things forward, to show them progress and they chose me. I'm going to build them a Sproatsville they'll be proud of.'

'So many strange faces, Ballbeagle, who are all these Polestars?'

'Never mind that Ripbag, I need you to register your arrival in this room with Malone, then you will be allocated specific mining rights.'

'Mining rights?' enquired Ripbag.

'Yes, but don't worry, you'll be more than happy with yours.'

Ballbeagle gave Ripbag a wry smile.

'Yes, I'm sure I will be,' replied Ripbag.

'Oh, the Auwnwanx,' said Ballbeagle. 'I take it you've remembered to bring the Auwnwanx with you for the Cassiopeia?'

'Oh yes, it's here,' said Ripbag.

'Would you like me to lock it away for you in my........ Ballbeagle hastily corrected himself, I mean *our* new secure facilities for safe keeping?'

'Oh no, Ballbeagle, as is my right and responsibility, I will bring it to the Cassiopeia and give it to Miranda who will of course present it to the new Polestar Prince or Princess.'

'Miranda!' squealed Ballbeagle. 'Is she here?'

'But of course,' replied Ripbag. 'Why? Does that give you a problem?'

'No, no of course not, good,' stuttered Ballbeagle. 'I'm sure she'll do a wonderful job. Well, I will have to get on, Ripbag, my ouzybag is looking rather flat. Good luck with your mining.'

Ballbeagle began to make his way out heading off towards Gatekeepers Lodge as Ripbag signed his entry in the new assignment book. A half smile passed across Ripbag's face momentarily as he noticed his old sparring partner, Jacadaro, had also arrived in Sproatsville. The plan to foil Ballbeagle's trickery and deceit had begun and the biggest battle in the history of Polestar and Welp conflict loomed ominously as Ripbag made his way back to Crooked Cottage.

Chapter Eleven

As predicted by the Council Heads, a massive fleet of Welp battleships had arrived on the edge of the Earth's atmosphere in preparation for an attack on Sproatsville. Unbeknown to Ripbag a small segment had broken off and landed in Blue Bell Wood unnoticed. This had all been pre-arranged with Ballbeagle and the presence of the Frombrasent Welps would further help to ensure that his fiendish plan to steal the Auwnwanx and rule Sproatsville would finally be realised. Once in their possession, a major part of the Welp fleet would descend upon Sproatsville, overpowering any resistance. With their fire power and the Auwnwanx at their disposal, they believed they were truly invincible.

After what seemed an eternity to most Polestars, the day of the Cassiopeia finally arrived and Conny Castle's extensive grounds had been suitably decorated and prepared to the highest of standards. Once again the place was buzzing with everyone looking forward to the sound of the flugelhorn, which would reverberate around Sproatsville at ten o'clock, signalling the start of this prestigious event.

During the run up to the Cassiopeia, Ripbag, Jacadaro, Morgan and Miranda had kept a very low profile and, apart from mining for Istella, had spent most of their days in Crooked Cottage with Smirnoff and Zalgud.

Smirnoff was all too aware of his responsibility to guard Zalgud, which he did faithfully, fearing repercussions from his ruling Council if she escaped. For this reason, Smirnoff would not take part in the Cassiopeia this year and he watched with envy through a gap in the slab as his four colleagues walked with hundreds of other Polestars up the hill towards Copper's Corner where the Scales of Justice had been assembled.

It was a wonderful sight with each and every Polestar's face glowing like a full moon on a clear dark night. Even Smirnoff, who was very much a loner, began to feel left out and for once in his life longed for acceptance and social interaction with other Polestars in the community. For the moment, however, his role was clearly defined.

On arriving at the top of the hill, Ripbag and his friends eventually caught first sight of Ballbeagle. He was standing on a platform acting as Master of Ceremonies just as Bullwrinkle used to do when directing and controlling affairs. Ripbag felt inclined to drag him off his soap box out of respect for Bullwrinkle but knew he had to remain focussed on the bigger plan and defend Sproatsville from the Frombrasent Welps. Stopping a short distance from where Ballbeagle stood, Miranda took a good look at his face.

'That's him, he's the one who persuaded me to intervene during Morgan's rescue.'

But before Ripbag could respond, Ballbeagle raised the flugelhorn to his mouth and the Cassiopeia began.

Polestars ran in all directions with ouzybags strapped to their sides hoping to find a good place to mine. Ripbag, Jacadaro, Morgan and Miranda followed suit. They knew the procedure and would have to return to the Scales of Justice no later than five minutes past midnight for the weigh-in. After which, the Polestar Prince or Princess elect would be carried shoulder high all the way to Conny Castle for the initiation ceremony.

Soon enough, if not too soon for some, the chimes from Swithun's Tower struck midnight and the harvesting was over. Polestars hastily made their way to the Scales of Justice, predictably some were purring outrageously at their yields and others looking dejected and miserable.

In turn, the Polestars placed their ouzybags onto the scales and watched as their weight was recorded on a board by Ballbeagle for all to see. As usual, Ripbag and Morgan had recorded decent weights with Jacadaro slightly in front of all other contenders. Then it was Miranda's turn. Ballbeagle had just chalked up the previous weight and was unaware of Miranda's presence at the scales.

'Hello, Ballbeagle,' she greeted, as he turned to face her.

'Oh err, hello Miranda,' he replied uncomfortably. 'Err, so pleased to see Morgan at this year's celebration and it's all down to you, I hear.'

'Yes, perhaps,' said Miranda, with a look of loathing on her face. 'Equally so, it's tragic that Wander is not here and that's down to you.'

Ballbeagle just stared at her, unable to find a suitable response as she turned away from him to join the hordes of Polestars waiting for the final result. Right at the back of the queue was Malone, the seedy little toad who allocated mining rights under the new regime.

Like Ballbeagle, he too came from Aldermin and, over recent months, had become one of his disciples, always by his side. Generally there was nothing worth discussing about Malone, he was a distant and unruly type with a greater reputation for wrong-doing than anything else. However, tonight was different because he was carrying three of the fattest ouzybags ever seen and the crowd drew to a hushed silence as he poured their contents onto the Scales of Justice. Ballbeagle was ecstatic.

'Thirty grams!' he screamed. 'Thirty grams!' 'Malone is our new Polestar Prince, hail Prince Malone, hail Prince Malone!'

Soon everyone joined in his chant and Malone was lifted shoulder high and carried along by scores of Polestars about to begin their journey to Conny Castle.

'Seems like you've been pipped at the post again, Jacadaro,' sympathised Ripbag.

'Yes and once again at the hands of a cheat' grimaced Jacadaro.

The result was no surprise to either of them really as they had a hunch that Ballbeagle would fix it, although they hadn't quite banked on Ballbeagle's foresight to install a representative of Aldermin as Polestar Prince which would give him easy access to the Auwnwanx. For the moment they would play along with Ballbeagle and joined the long, winding procession which illuminated the back road to the Castle under a blanket of beautiful twinkling stars.

By the time Ripbag and his friends reached Conny Castle, Malone was sitting firmly on the Polestar scales watching those who had taken part in the Cassiopeia donate ouzybags into the opposite bowl. Deep resentment was etched on Jacadaro's face when his turn came to donate. He'd already been robbed by Malone once and rewarding him further with a gift of his own Istella was a double hit. Nevertheless, he did so and joined Ripbag, Morgan and Miranda, who were reluctantly, but enthusiastically, taking part in the games and celebrations of the Cassiopeia including the infamous Big Dipper!

Eventually, on a tide of euphoria and jubilation, Malone was carried triumphantly to the throne of the new Polestar Prince and once in place sat somewhat majestically awaiting the greatest prize of all, the Auwnwanx.

This was the moment all Polestars dreamed of and everyone rushed forward to watch the presentation, which was to be directed by Ballbeagle. When all the mayhem had died down and order had been restored, Ballbeagle turned to face Ripbag.

'Well Ripbag, we're waiting,' he said.

'Waiting,' replied Ripbag.

'Yes,' snapped Ballbeagle irritably. 'The Auwnwanx, I take it you have it?'

Ripbag didn't respond to Ballbeagle's comment but slowly took off his jacket, which brought gasps of delight and admiration from the crowd. To ensure its safety whilst in his possession, Ripbag had wrapped the Auwnwanx around his shoulders and waist and the whole body of this beautiful creature was bursting with colour in recognition of the Cassiopeia and its destiny to serve the winner.

Ripbag unwrapped the Auwnwanx from his torso and carefully handed it to Miranda, the youngest female Polestar on assignment in Sproatsville, who would present it to Malone.

With the Auwnwanx draped over her arms, Miranda made her way forward and placed the beautiful creature on Malone's lap. Tumultuous cheers and applause erupted from all those present, everyone that is except Ripbag, Morgan, Jac and Miranda. Seizing his moment, Ballbeagle screamed at the top of his voice, 'Sproatsville has a new Polestar Prince, let celebrations continue in recognition of Prince Malone.'

The noise was deafening as Ballbeagle whipped up the crowd's enthusiasm to a crescendo, so much so that no one had even noticed that the Auwnwanx's beautiful glow had all but died away, perhaps entirely due to the dubious character of the recipient and the circumstances in which he became Polestar Prince.

Ripbag quickly gathered Morgan, Jac and Miranda together.

'OK, listen up everyone, it seems the Heads of Council were right about Ballbeagle's intention to take possession of the Auwnwanx early during the Cassiopeia and our plan to foil him must not fail. He is already heading towards Blue Bell Wood and I must follow him. Miranda, you will come with me, Jac and Morgan make sure you don't lose sight of Malone and the Auwnwanx. Track him wherever he goes.'

'What about the Frombrasent Welps, Ripbag, are they here?' 'Will they attack?'

'I don't know, Morgan,' said Ripbag. 'If all goes to plan, the combined forces of the Polestars will now be in place, to intercept any threat from the Welps. This will be the battle of all battles but there is nothing we can do to affect that, we must succeed in our task here.'

With that, Ripbag and Miranda set off in pursuit of Ballbeagle, heading towards Bluebell Wood with trepidation, as this was the domain of Red Snapper, the mutant, who had terrorised Polestars in Sproatsville for many years and who was responsible for Morgan's recent capture and imprisonment. For this reason,

Ripbag avoided asking Morgan to accompany him and chose Miranda instead.

Keen to keep track on Malone's movements, Jac and Morgan returned to the celebrations. Malone was the centre of attention, lapping it up, boasting about his cache of Istella and his status as Polestar Prince which guaranteed him fame and fortune back on Aldermin. Jac's stomach was churning, knowing full well he was a fraud and a cheat but, in true Jacadaro style, he remained cool and unruffled.

Some time later, Morgan tapped Jac on the shoulder, drawing his attention towards Malone, who had gradually separated himself from the main gathering of Polestars and was quietly edging away. Sure enough and very slowly, Malone became more and more distant until his absence was unnoticed by those revellers still engrossed in true Cassiopeia fever. Quickly, but stealthily, Jac and Morgan began to track him, as he predictably headed off in the same direction as Ballbeagle to the notorious Bluebell Wood.

'Are you going to be OK with this?' asked Jac as they made their way, being aware of Morgan's terrifying experience with Red Snapper.

After a short pause, Morgan smiled and replied, 'Are you?' Reminding Jac that he too had been unlucky enough to make her acquaintance.

'Then let's get to it,' said Jac as they took a wide berth enabling them to ambush Malone in total surprise.

Chapter Twelve

Breathless and bedraggled, Malone eventually entered the outskirts of Bluebell Wood. Looking nervous and uneasy, he clutched the Auwnwanx tightly inwardly praying that it would somehow protect him from the jaws of Red Snapper. His glow had faded, but for some reason not totally, as he crept wearily through the dense foliage that cluttered the ground before him. He was sure that beyond every tree and bush he could see ghouls and Welps and, dare he even say it, Red herself, but he continued knowing he was near his journey's end.

'Can't be long now, can't be long now,' he kept repeating to himself. 'Must keep going, I'm Polestar Prince, I can do anything. The Auwnwanx protects the Polestar Prince so it is going to protect me.'

Malone really was terrified. He had lost all sense of verbal reasoning and was bordering on gibberish, saying anything to convince himself he would be OK. He reached a clearing in the wood which required him to take a sharp left onto the long, but narrow pathway which led to an old abandoned tractor.

The tractor had been discarded many years ago by the humans and was a known landmark to Polestars. Malone took the turning but was stopped in his tracks by the most blinding, dazzling light he had ever seen, so bright he could feel its heat radiating off his body. 'Aaahhh' he cried out shielding his eyes with his hands. 'What's that?'

Malone could hear the crushing and splitting of crops all around him and the ground shuddered with perfect timing each and every second. It was getting closer, louder and stronger until it was almost upon him.

'What's happening?' he cried. 'Someone help me please.' And then............ nothing, just pure silence.

The bright light had disappeared and his body no longer warmed by its source. The ground was once again stable. Malone remained still but for his trembling. He felt sure his worst nightmare was about to be realised knowing full well he'd been playing in Red Snapper's back garden, but still nothing more than silence.

Ever so slowly Malone lowered his hands from his eyes. Gradually raising his head to look forward he couldn't make anything out at first as the bright light had temporarily affected his sight. But, like a binocular wheel turning, his vision adjusted to reveal the enormous head of a human with bulging, bloodshot eyes staring straight at him. Malone took a deep intake of breath and fell backwards in horror to the ground. This wasn't his worst nightmare but it certainly came close. He tried in vain to become invisible by losing his glow but it just didn't work, in fact he began to glow brighter and brighter making himself more and more visible.

'Hello, little man' said the human, menacingly, his chin resting firmly on the ground.

'At last we meet again.'

'Mmmmad Pete,' stuttered Malone pushing himself tentatively away.

'Yes, Mad Pete,' he replied. 'Only beforehand I was simply known as Pete to folk around here, that is until you lot changed things.'

'Wwwwhat do you want?' asked Malone, still backtracking.

'What do I want? Oh that's easy, little man. I want my mind back, and you, you're my ticket to sanity.'

Mad Pete suddenly lunged forward in an attempt to grab him but before he could reach him, Malone was pulled into the undergrowth by Jacadaro. Both Morgan and Jacadaro had caught up with Malone and had been observing his encounter with Mad Pete invisibly and therefore in safety.

'Get in here, you idiot,' exclaimed Jacadaro. Malone tucked in close by Jacadaro's side and inexplicably lost his entire glow becoming invisible. Wasting no time, all three Polestars headed off on the long narrow footpath out of harms way.

'Come back, come back do you hear,' screamed Mad Pete searching furiously on all fours.

'I know you exist, I'm not mad. I'll find you one day, come back.' His voice was fading however as the distance between him and the Polestars grew greater and greater.

Eventually they stopped running and Mad Pete was no where to be seen. Jacadaro couldn't contain his anger and grabbed hold of Malone by his collar.

'Well Malone, got yourself lost did you? Cassiopeia not exciting enough? Just thought you'd take a stroll in Bluebell Wood, eh?'

'I don't have to answer to you, Jacadaro, I can go where I like, when I like, I'm Polestar Prince remember?'

'Ah yes, that enchanting title that somehow keeps evading me, due to scummy low lives like you,' replied Jac. 'Haven't you wondered why you remained visible in Mad Pete's presence? The Auwnwanx will always work against you.'

Jac withdrew one of his plectrone blades from its sheath in anger.

Morgan intervened, 'No! Stop!' he cried

'Malone will be dealt with by the Heads of Council, and until then he remains in one piece, Jac, understand?'

'But of course,' Jac replied, in a superior tone, as he slowly replaced the weapon.

'Regretfully Malone, not only must I spare your life but I have to wear your stinky clothes, which consequently damages my reputation far more than failure to cut you into tiny pieces! Nevertheless needs must, take them off!'

Malone dare not resist and in no time he and Jacadaro had exchanged their clothes. Although this wasn't the time for humour, Morgan couldn't help but smile seeing the dapper Jacadaro looking like a tramp and Malone bursting out of cool clobber two sizes too small for him. Morgan was careful not to upset Jac any further however and instead focused his attention upon the next task at hand.

Turning to Malone, Morgan asked 'Where are you expected to rendezvous with Ballbeagle?'

'Ballbeagle?' repeated Malone. 'Don't know what you're talking about.'

'For a Polestar Prince, you really lack sincerity, Malone.' We know all about

Ballbeagle and his plan to rule Sproatsville. We know all about the Frombrasent Welps' desire to possess the Auwnwanx and we know all about Aldermin's involvement in this. Now I'll ask you once more, where were you going to meet Ballbeagle?'

Malone remained silent.

'Right, then we'll just have to find him ourselves. Tie him up, Jac.'

Jacadaro pinned Malone to a tall thin stem of a blue bell flower, which heavily populated the wood, securing him firmly in place.

'Good luck,' said Morgan. 'I understand Red Snapper loves her bait presented on a skewer.'

Turning away, he and Jac headed for the dense network of trees, dark passages and furrows.

'No, no you can't leave me here, come back, come back!' screamed Malone. But to no avail. A sense of panic raced through his body as he fought in vain to release himself from the grapple whips which secured him.

'OK, OK, I'll tell you, just don't leave me here!'

Jac and Morgan returned quickly to cut Malone free. This time they found him more than willing to divulge the vital information they needed.

'It's the clearing where the old tractor lies, I'm to meet Ballbeagle there with the Auwnwanx. He promised I would receive Istella for the rest of my life if I agreed to help.'

'And you didn't even think to ask why?' said Morgan. 'You're an even bigger fool than I had you down for.'

'Yeah, save it for your trial, Malone,' said Jac. 'Come on Morgan, we need to make tracks.'

'What are we going to do with him?' asked Morgan, looking directly at Malone. Jac suddenly realised that Malone couldn't be left to make his way back to the Cassiopeia, as he was going to be a vital witness in Ballbeagle's downfall.

'We have no choice,' he said. 'One of us will have to escort him back to secure detention, and as I'm dressed in his clothes right now, it will have to be you, Morgan.'

Morgan knew this made sense and handed Jacadaro the Auwnwanx.

'Good luck my friend and keep your eyes peeled.'

'Thanks, I will,' replied Jac, as he turned and disappeared into the dark crevasses of the wood.

'Don't hang around here, Morgan, do you understand, be on your way,' warned Jac. 'Make tracks now.'

But there was no response from Morgan, not because he was in jeopardy but because he, more than anyone else, understood the dangers present in Bluebell Wood and he'd already left.

Jac was now alone and had to find his way to the old tractor. With the Auwnwanx firmly in his grip, he crept stealthily in and out of the dense foliage and water-logged terrain fearing the worst at every turn. At last he caught sight of the old tractor and the unscrupulous Ballbeagle eagerly awaiting Malone, his accomplice and accessory.

Jac drew breath and sat with his back pushed hard against a large unearthed tree. He had no idea where Ripbag and Miranda were, whether they had come to any harm or whether Ballbeagle was alone. He knew, however, that he couldn't stay where he was and at some point would need to approach Ballbeagle in his disguise.

Jac crouched keeping his head low, and began to make his way towards Ballbeagle. Malone always wore a hood and this enabled Jac to shield his face until he came within touching distance of Ballbeagle. Jac could see he was getting closer and closer and wasn't sure how events would unfold in the next few moments. Suddenly he was there.

Purr, purr…….'Thank goodness,' said Ballbeagle. 'Thank goodness you're here, what on earth kept you? I thought you'd had second thoughts.'

Jac didn't respond and could now make Ballbeagle out under the clear light of the moon.

'Well come on Malone, hand it over, the Auwnwanx, give it here.'

Jac didn't take kindly to these words as it seemed everyone wanted to take the Auwnwanx from him, usually in dishonest circumstances. Slowly raising his hands, Jac lifted the hood away from his head revealing his unmistakable quiff. Ballbeagle stepped back in shock, inhaling deeply.

'Jacadaro!' he exclaimed. 'What are you doing here, where is Malone?'

'Oh he's probably a little tied up right now,' replied Ripbag, stepping out with Miranda from behind the trees. Ballbeagle spun on his heels to face Ripbag realising that his plan to steal the Auwnwanx had been exposed and he was now in grave danger.

'How yer doing buddy?' said Ripbag somewhat menacingly. 'Isn't it weird, don't you think, how you always seem to be in the strangest of places without good reason? That time when you scared the glow out of me near Gatekeepers Lodge, for example, and then there was our chance meeting in Swampy when I stumbled across the Frombrasent Welps, not to mention the kind considerate Polestar who gave Miranda the benefit of his advice, even if it was for selfish reasons. Any of this ringing true, Ballbeagle?' asked Ripbag.

Ballbeagle didn't respond, he just stared at Ripbag with a contemptuous, if not defiant, smirk on his face.

'And lo and behold, here we are again,' said Ripbag. 'In another of your strange places.'

'What a fool, what a fool I've been,' said Ripbag. 'But then again, you don't expect so-called friends to be double crossing snakes, do you?'

'Come come, Ripbag, you're not averse to the betterment that power and control can bring you,' said Ballbeagle. 'Join me, we would make a great team. You wouldn't just be Polestar Prince for a year you could be Ripbag, joint ruler of Sproatsville, custodian of all the Istella fields, the most powerful Polestar ever. What do you think?'

'I must admit, Ballbeagle, you make the offer sound very attractive but for two things. One, I'm not the scum bag you've turned out to be, and two, you took away from me the most beautiful thing in the whole universe, her name was Wander, and for that I'm going to give you a choice Ballbeagle.'

Ripbag drew his plectrone blades from their holsters and lowered them to his side.

'You can face me in a duel to the death in memory of her name or you can stand trial on Vega, her star - you choose.'

'Actually, Ripbag, there is a third choice,' replied Ballbeagle.

'Oh really?' enquired Ripbag.

'Yes I could simply ask these Welps to tear you limb from limb.'

In his quest to avenge Wander's death or to bring Ballbeagle to justice on Vega, Ripbag had failed to notice the arrival of six heavily armed Frombrasent Welps deployed from the small fleet which had landed in Bluebell Wood. They were there to receive the Auwnwanx from Ballbeagle and their timing prompted howls of laughter from him as he realised the balance of power had swung heavily in his favour.

'You see, Ripbag, purr purr.... I'm destined to rule Sproatsville and not even a pleb like you can do anything to stop me.'

'Oh, how I've despised you over the years, always yearning to be the respected one, beating me at everything, ridiculing me because of my physique and stature, but not any more Ripbag. Ballbeagle and the ruling Council of Aldermin will share the recognition we rightfully deserve only you and your band of merry men won't be around to see it. Ballbeagle stepped forward and snatched the Auwnwanx from Jacadaro.

'The final piece in the jigsaw,' he whispered. He turned to the leader of the Welps troop.

'Give me a few moments to reach the safety of your battleships and then kill them all,' he instructed.

Ballbeagle took one last look at Ripbag, smiled and then disappeared into the woods.

The Frombrasent Welps removed all weaponry from the captive Polestars and ordered them to turn around and stand close together. Miranda's knees were knocking as she realised that her life was in danger but she was determined to show courage and would not demean herself by pleading for mercy from the aggressors. Ripbag and Jac remained helplessly silent.

'Take aim,' ordered the commander of the Welps, and then................. nothing, absolutely nothing happened. Ripbag, Jac and Miranda were rooted to the spot waiting for the command to 'fire' but nothing more was said. Slowly the three turned their heads to look behind them. To their astonishment the Welps were standing to attention looking straight ahead with weapons by their sides, but now they numbered seven. They had been joined by another one of their kind, it was Zalgud. Her timely appearance and obvious high profile had frozen proceedings. The troop hardly dare move.

'Zalgud!' gasped Ripbag.

'Yes,' she replied as she beckoned Smirnoff to join his Polestar colleagues.

'Really, Ripbag, you should have left someone far more competent than Smirnoff to guard me, but nevertheless I'm grateful for your naivety.'

Poor Smirnoff was once again left feeling he had let the side down. Zalgud had cunningly disarmed Smirnoff of his HIT gun and then used it to free herself from her retaining shackles. Smirnoff had been forced to take her to Bluebell Wood where she knew her battle fleet would be assembled. Turning to her foot soldiers, Zalgud ordered them back to the fleet immediately to prepare for her return, claiming that the killing of these particular Polestars would be her pleasure and her pleasure alone. Not daring to question her wisdom, the foot soldiers immediately obeyed her orders and left the scene.

'Turn around,' she demanded looking straight at Ripbag.

Once again the brave Polestars obeyed the command. A few short moments passed and then four shots blasted out from the HIT gun which she had taken from Smirnoff, but amazingly they were left unharmed.

'Stay exactly where you are,' said Zalgud, as she walked slowly towards them.

'And now, Smirnoff,' she whispered in his ear. 'I have repaid you for saving my life, from here on we owe each other nothing, absolutely nothing, do you understand?'

'Yes,' whimpered Smirnoff, but when he turned around to acknowledge Zalgud she had gone and was heading for the safety of her fleet. Miranda held her head in her hands.

'Are you OK?' asked Ripbag, realising that this must have been a terrifying experience for her, if not them all.

'Yes, I'll be fine,' she said. 'I just can't believe that we've survived two executions in as many minutes!'

'We must find Ballbeagle,' said Ripbag. 'We have no time to lose, the Auwnwanx must not get into the hands of the Welps.'

Realising the urgency behind Ripbag's comment, they all set off after Ballbeagle.

It was no secret that Ballbeagle was cumbersome and in Ripbag's opinion would not have travelled too far. Suddenly Ballbeagle came into view heading towards one of the Welp's ships and, without hesitation, Smirnoff put his foot on the gas leaving the others in a cloud of dust, bringing Ballbeagle to the ground by the banks of Bluebell Lake. Moments later Ripbag, Jacadaro and Miranda arrived at the scene.

'Give me the Auwnwanx, Ballbeagle,' demanded Ripbag, with his arms outstretched.

'No way,' countered Ballbeagle looking ruffled and breathless. 'It's mine, do you hear, mine, Sproatsville is mine, it is my destiny.'

'Hand it over,' insisted Jacadaro. 'Do it and you'll be free to leave with the Welps.'

'Fools the lot of you,' retorted Ballbeagle. 'I don't need your blessing for anything. I make the decisions around here, not you.' Ballbeagle produced a HIT gun and aimed it straight at Ripbag.

'Losers!' he scowled. 'I should have done the job earlier myself, however the pleasure is now all mine.'

Ballbeagle was the blink of an eye away from pulling the trigger when out from the depths of the lake leaped the hugely grotesque and awesome Red Snapper, taking hold of Ballbeagle firmly in her jaws.

The young Polestars fell back and screamed in horror as Ballbeagle's cries penetrated the whole of Bluebell Wood, but he was beyond help. Without warning Miranda dashed forward towards Ballbeagle, once again putting her own life at risk, just as she had done when Morgan was a mutant.

'No Miranda,' yelled Ripbag. 'He's not worth it, come back!'

But the gritty Polestar remained unperturbed. Within striking distance of Red Snapper, she dived to the ground and grasped the Auwnwanx, which Ballbeagle had dropped in his desperate, if not futile, battle for his life.

Miranda wasn't interested in Ballbeagle at all it was the Auwnwanx she wanted and as quickly as she had retrieved it, she then retreated to the safety of cover behind the trees. Turning around, the last they all saw of Ballbeagle was his feet disappearing slowly over the bank of the lake into its murky depths.

'Over here, Miranda, quickly over here!' screamed Ripbag. All three Polestars headed for an area away from where Red Snapper had appeared just in case she decided to return and crouched low together in the undergrowth to evade detection. There was a notable droning sound reverberating all around them and it was getting louder and louder.

'Look,' said Smirnoff. 'Look over there.' Smirnoff was pointing towards the stars and when Ripbag and Miranda followed his path they could see the dark sky littered with hundreds of Polestar battleships. The combined forces of Polaris, Alrai, Vega, Thurban and Kochab had arrived led by Manangos.

Immediately the engines of the Welps battleships fired up and they slowly hovered a short distance above the ground. Zalgud could be seen clearly at the controls of the lead ship. She had caught sight of Smirnoff, who was watching her ship gain height. He was mesmerised by the stunning lights and grace of these powerful awesome crafts and eventually stood to his feet in full view of Zalgud. Smirnoff knew he could be taken out easily and his behaviour at any other time would be considered foolish but somehow none of that seemed to matter. Out of respect and defiance, he raised his hand acknowledging Zalgud, who remained unmoved.

The light in the craft dimmed and they disappeared into space joining the rest of the Welp fleet. They were not a match for the massive force of Polestar battleships and their expected destination was Aldermin.

Chapter Thirteen

Ripbag, Jac and Miranda joined Smirnoff staring deep into the night.

'We did it.'

'What was that Smirnoff?' asked Ripbag.

'We did it,' he replied. 'We scuppered Ballbeagle's plan, saved Sproatsville from the Welps, retrieved the Auwnwanx and I'm a free Polestar, we did it!'

Smirnoff turned to face the others and for the first time in his life his smile lit up half of Bluebell Wood. Smirnoff's excitement was infectious and in no time at all four Polestars were holding hands, skipping in circles and screaming in jubilation. Ripbag couldn't ever remember hearing Smirnoff purr before but he was leading the way in this quartet. They had forgotten all about Red Snapper and that they had escaped with their lives by a whisker only moments earlier and Ripbag, well he was drinking with the Gods now the Auwnwanx was back in his possession and firmly wrapped around his shoulders.

The dance continued round and round spinning like a wheel and nobody wanted it to stop except for Ripbag who suddenly realised that the Auwnwanx had begun to glow a deep red colour.

'Wow,' Ripbag yelled, as he hauled the Auwnwanx from around his neck and threw it to the ground.

'It's hot,' he yelped.   'It's burning hot.' Everyone stopped and stared deep into the mass of this magical mysterious creature, watching as its body began to break up into a carpet of the most beautiful burning embers lighting up their faces.

'What's happening?' asked Miranda.

'I don't know,' replied Jac.   'But don't get too close,' he warned.

'It's Bullwrinkle,' said Ripbag.   'It's what he said to me on his death bed.' Jac, Smirnoff and Miranda looked at Ripbag inquisitively.   He seemed totally mesmerised by what was happening.

'I've never understood what he meant but it all seems to make sense now.   *He who dances with fire will truly receive his greatest desire.*' That is why the Welps desperately wanted to steal the Auwnwanx, to dance in its flames and fulfil their greatest desire to rule over all Polestars.   When the Auwnwanx is not presented to the rightful Polestar Prince or Princess it transforms into a carpet of flames. Dance in the flames of the Auwnwanx and its prophecy is realised.   Ballbeagle and the Welps must have known that the inauguration of

Malone as Polestar Prince would enable them access to the prophecy and for their greatest desires to be met. Bullwrinkle needed to share his secret knowledge with me. He knew one day I would dance amongst the flames, I'm sure of it.'

'You, dance amongst the flames?' repeated Jacadaro. 'Are you mad?'

Ripbag was undeterred by Jac's response and, without looking down, began to walk slowly towards the embers, which had turned to burning hot glowing coals.

'Ripbag!' screamed Miranda. 'Come back, what are you doing?'

But Jac held Miranda's arm firmly.

'Don't interfere, Miranda, leave him, leave him be.'

Ripbag maintained his course until eventually his stride landed him deep in the flames of the Auwnwanx. Unbelievably, he came to no harm. He seemed immune to the fierce heat.

Ripbag's friends could hardly believe their eyes. The heat was so intense they were forced to move back, yet there was Ripbag standing right in the heart of it. He began to dance outrageously, producing tongues of fire and plumes of smoke from beneath his tiny bopping feet. Jac was gob-smacked, he had never seen such moves. Then came the singing, with his arms reaching out to the stars.

'He who, dan-ces with fire, will tru-ly receive, his great-est desire. He who, dan-ces with fire, will tru-ly receive, his great-est desire.'

Constantly repeating this line, he gyrated amongst the burning hot coals until finally, through exhaustion, he could perform no more.

'Please grant me my wish,' he gasped as he collapsed to his knees. 'Bring Wander back to me and my old friend and guardian Bullwrinkle, even for a short while.'

Jac, Smirnoff and Miranda could hardly hold back their tears as Ripbag's unusual behaviour suddenly had real meaning. He looked a pitiful sight and it was obvious his heart was still broken over the loss of his friend and guardian, Bullwrinkle, and his secret love, Wander. He hoped the prophecy of the Auwnwanx would put all of this right enabling him to fulfil his greatest desire, but it was not to be. Jac and Miranda moved to help Ripbag to his feet.

'Come on, buddy,' Jac said, putting his arm around Ripbag's shoulders. 'Let's go home.'

Miranda threw her arms around Ripbag's waist.

'We all love you Ripbag, we always will.'

A few moments passed without word from anyone and then they slowly began to make their way out of the woods, arms interlocked in unity and support.

Ripbag suddenly stopped.

'Wait, we can't leave the remains of the Auwnwanx here,' he said. 'We must gather up the coals in our ouzybags and take them back to the Cassiopeia, at least then I can explain what happened to the Heads of Council.'

In full agreement, they turned to make their way back to the Auwnwanx. Kneeling down, they began to gather the charred coals into a small pile, and proceeded to build a sizeable column resembling a cairn on a mountain top.

'Have we got it all?' asked Ripbag.

'Yes, I think so,' replied Miranda. 'They need to cool a little more though as they are starting to smoke.'

A line of smoke was indeed rising slowly from the top of the stack, meandering side-to-side until it faded away. This was a strange occurrence, as the coals had already cooled considerably but the smoke was getting thicker and thicker, turning pure white. The Polestars began to push themselves away by the heels of their feet, putting distance between them and this puzzling phenomenon. The smoke began to form shapes swirling, dancing and turning within itself, but it no longer disappeared into thin air.

'What have you done, Ripbag?' screamed Jac. 'Iris, the winged Goddess of the Rainbow, has sent demons to punish us. You shouldn't have messed with the Auwnwanx, you have offended her.'

'Wait,' said Miranda. 'Look, look!'

The smoke had turned brilliant white and had worked itself into a ghostly apparition of a Polestar. Eerily, the hand of the apparition reached out towards Ripbag, which was all Smirnoff needed for him to disappear behind a tree. He wanted nothing to do with it. He was scared and considered himself in more danger than anything he'd experienced on Capper. Ripbag, however, was mesmerised and gradually plucked up the courage to reach out towards the delicate beckoning hand until eventually their fingertips touched.

Immediately the smoke was sucked deep into the coals to reveal the slender and beautiful figure of Wander. The inconceivable and unimaginable expressions on Jacadaro and Miranda's faces were only upstaged by the look of disbelief from Ripbag.

'Is, is it really you Wander? Are you for real?' stammered Ripbag.

Wander stepped forward without taking her gaze away from Ripbag and slowly knelt down in front of him. She reached into the tiny pocket of her gown and retrieved a small object, which she clenched tightly in her fist. Taking hold of Ripbag's hand, she deposited the object. It was the small beautifully decorated note that Ripbag had returned to her on that fateful day during Morgan's rescue. Ripbag opened it carefully to reveal its contents. He read out loud, 'Together we will never be alone'.

'It is you, Wander, you are for real, you're alive!'

'Yes,' squealed Wander. 'By the grace of the Auwnwanx.'

They fell together in each others arms, hugging and squeezing each other, hardly daring to let go, in case it was all just a dream. But it wasn't, Wander was for real and the Auwnwanx had delivered its prophecy.

Eventually, Smirnoff came out from his hiding. He joined Jac and Miranda, with Ripbag and Wander in the greatest huddle of all time. Miranda was almost inconsolable bearing in mind the feeling of guilt she had carried since Wander's regrettable death. Now she could forget all of that, as they all could and put it behind them.

'Come on,' said Jac. 'Let's get out of this place. We have things to celebrate, we must go to the Cassiopeia.'

'Yes,' said Ripbag. 'But we must collect all the remains of the Auwnwanx first.'

Everyone agreed but as they turned to gather them up, their eyes grew wide in amazement. The Auwnwanx had transformed itself into the beautiful creature it had always been, awaiting its presentation to the next Polestar Prince or Princess. Smiles of joy lit up everyone's faces.

Ripbag picked up the Auwnwanx, secured it firmly around his shoulders, turned towards Smirnoff and said, 'Lead us out of here, my friend, by the quickest path you know.'

Smirnoff needed no encouragement and soon the group were well on their way out of the dark and dangerous wood on route to the Cassiopeia. As they left, Ripbag looked back at the scene and reflected upon the miracle that had occurred. He couldn't help feeling a little disappointed that his desire to see his old friend Bullwrinkle again had not been granted.

Ripbag remembered Bullwrinkle's words on that fateful day *Until we meet again,* and his eyes scanned the dark holes created by the branches and leaves of the trees, but still there was nothing. One day we'll meet again, Bullwrinkle, one day, I know it, he said to himself.

When the group reached the safety of Conny Castle they encountered a spectacle like they had never seen before. Scores of Polestars were patrolling the grounds, with hundreds of battleships hovering above. The long walkway to Conny Castle was lined with heavily armed Polestars, some of them looking seriously mean, especially the ones from Alrai, who stood out a mile.

'Let them through,' voices urged. 'Move aside.'

Eventually they made their way to the centre stage of the Cassiopeia. As the crowd caught sight of Ripbag holding the Auwnwanx, and then Wander and the others, the place erupted.

Burly guards struggled to maintain the pathway up to the Heads of Council, as everyone wanted to touch and greet their heroes. They were all aware of the skulduggery and antics led by Ballbeagle, and all of those who had assisted in his outrageous plans including Malone were in custody.

As the group approached the platform where the Heads of Council were assembled, Manangos rose from his seat, raised his hand high and commanded silence. The huge crowd came to a swift hush.

'Today,' he began, 'one of our own tried to procure the Auwnwanx into the hands of our arch enemy, the Frombrasent Welps. He did this to fuel his greed for power and to control the distribution of Istella, the most important resource in the universe. Today he failed and the reason he failed is all around us, a united and unshakable camaraderie to defend ourselves against evil. Driven by immense bravery and courage, the kind shown by Ripbag and his friends, Ballbeagle, the Welps and those who dare to threaten us should know that tomorrow they will all fail again, we will never be defeated.'

Cheers and applause echoed out from the Cassiopeia, not only in recognition of Manangos' rousing words of leadership, but also out of gratitude to Ripbag, Jacadaro, Smirnoff, Morgan and Miranda. Manangos raised his hand again.

'Thanks to these brave Polestars, the Auwnwanx is back where it belongs, at the Cassiopeia and today it must be presented to a new Polestar Prince or Princess, a genuine contender, who rightly deserves such accolade.'

Manangos lifted the Auwnwanx from Ripbag's shoulders and asked Miranda to step forward. Nervously, the young female from Vega approached the mighty Manangos who reassured her and placed the Auwnwanx in her hands. Manangos whispered into Miranda's ear. She grinned, relaxed and stepped lightly forward until she stood before the cool, but inquisitive Jacadaro.

'Is there anyone here who would deny Jacadaro the honour of becoming Polestar Prince?' asked Manangos.

'No, no,' returned the crowd.

'Then so be it.'

Miranda leaned forward giggling with delight and placed the Auwnwanx over Jac's shoulders. He was immediately hoisted high in the air by Ripbag, Smirnoff and Morgan who then planted him firmly on the throne. He had finally achieved what had been rightfully his on two previous occasions and he was overwhelmed. So too was Rosco, the head of Kochab, whose chest was stuck so far out it looked fit to explode. He was so proud of Jacadaro and welcomed the esteem the Auwnwanx would bring to his own powerful and respected star

Finally came the most important endorsement of the night. The Auwnwanx burst into colour, flickering its many beautiful eyes. The scene couldn't have been more perfect. Jac was Polestar Prince, the Auwnwanx was safe and in its rightful place and Wander was once again by Ripbag's side. This was going to be the Cassiopeia of all Cassiopeias and that's exactly how it turned out to be purr .... fect.

Sproatsville was a much safer and happier place now, despite the constant threat from Red Snapper and the Frombrasent Welps and life had returned to normal with the mining of Istella being the focus of all those who visited this extraordinary village.

No one knew for sure whether Ballbeagle escaped the clutches of Red Snapper, but the signs certainly didn't look good for him. As for the Welps, their course to Aldermin was of concern to everyone and the prospects for peace and security throughout the Polestar communities looked more fragile than ever before.

When the next lunation of the moon arrived, Ripbag, Smirnoff, Morgan, Wander and Miranda were all ready for the return journey to Polaris through the gravity corridor. They had gathered at Swampy, although on this occasion, thankfully, not in the middle of it. Smirnoff would fly to Alrai from Polaris using one of the many supply ships and he couldn't wait. Previously he had left Sproatsville as a criminal but was returning to Alrai a hero. Wander was excited, she would be fulfilling her wish to return to Polaris with Ripbag, only this time in far happier circumstances.

The proudest Polestar however had to be Jacadaro. Rosco, the Head of the Ruling

Council on Kochab, had decided that he would take Jac back in his personal battleship as reward for becoming Polestar Prince. Jac couldn't wait to see the faces of his family and friends back on Kochab when he touched down with Rosco at the controls and the Auwnwanx by his side. This would do no harm to his cool reputation whatsoever and he loved it.

'It's nearly time to go,' said Morgan. 'I can feel the pull on my shoulders and my feet are getting lighter.'

'You're right,' said Ripbag. 'Come on everyone, let's touch hands.'

The five Polestars stood in a line looking back towards the centre of Sproatsville. They giggled and purred as they waited for the gravity corridor to take them. The glow from their faces illuminated Swampy and you could see similar scenes all over Sproatsville from other returning Polestars too, but none of them achieved the glow of these Polestars, who must have been the happiest around!

'Wow, here it comes!' screamed Miranda. 'Hold tight everyone.'

'See you back on Polaris,' said Morgan, as they were launched with such force that five pairs of Polestar boots were left on the spot where they stood! Their stay on Sproatsville during this lunation phase had finally come to an end.

Walking along the main road in Sproatsville, a little girl holding her mother's hand pointed towards the sky and said, 'Mummy look, what's that?'

Reassuringly her mother replied, 'It's a shooting star, Winnie. How lucky you are to have seen one.'

'What's a shooting star?' asked the little girl.

'Shooting stars are tiny rocks travelling through space leaving a trail of light burning behind them. They are beautiful, aren't they?'

For the little girl, this was perhaps a plausible explanation for what she had just seen, however you now know the truth behind such phenomena in our skies and the incredible goings on in the extraordinary village of Sproatsville.